"I'm sorry," she said. "I just wish we could both go back to last year and...I don't know, run away together."

He nodded. "I'd go this time. But now I wish a lot of things."

"What, Colt?"

"That I could sleep through the night. That I didn't break out in a sweat when I get into a car. That I could be around my brothers without wanting to press my hands to my ears and run in the opposite direction. And most of all, I wish I could have been here to protect you."

"I wish I could have been there to protect you, too, Colt."

They stared at each other across the vast expanse of the few feet that separated them. She still wanted to leave. He still wanted to stay. And neither of them would ever be the same again.

TRIBAL BLOOD

JENNA KERNAN

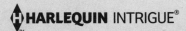

For Jim, always

ISBN-13: 978-1-335-52632-8

Tribal Blood

Copyright © 2018 by Jeannette H. Monaco

Recycling programs for this product may not exist in your area.

Printed in U.S.A.

Jenna Kernan has penned over two dozen novels and has received two RITA® Award nominations. Jenna is every bit as adventurous as her heroines. Her hobbies include recreational gold prospecting, scuba diving and gem hunting. Jenna grew up in the Catskills and currently lives in the Hudson Valley in New York State with her husband. Follow Jenna on Twitter, @jennakernan, on Facebook or at jennakernan.com.

Books by Jenna Kernan

Visit the Author Profile page at Harlequin.com.

CAST OF CHARACTERS

Colt Redhorse—A rescued prisoner of war who recently returned to Turquoise Canyon. His time as an enemy captive has scarred him and he now lives in seclusion and will speak to no one but his brother Ty. He tried to see Kacey on his return but found her gone.

Kacey Doka—She begged Colt not to join the service and planned to leave after he shipped out, but instead was kidnapped first. She's escaped and is on the run.

Jake Redhorse—The newest hire on the Turquoise Canyon Tribal Police force. He has tried and failed to see Colt on several occasions since Colt's return.

Lori Mott—Colt's new sister-in-law and a nurse at the tribe's health clinic. She would like to get Colt into the hospital for evaluation.

Ty Redhorse—Colt's older brother who served his country with honor and seems to have no PTSD. He has gang ties and a troubling past but he has always been there for Colt.

Kee Redhorse—The oldest of Colt's brothers and a physician at the tribe's clinic who wants to get Colt psychiatric help. Colt disappears each time he has come looking for him.

Jack Bear Den—A Turquoise Guardian and the tribe's only detective.

Wallace Tinnin—Chief of the tribal police force.

Dr. Hector Hauser—The director of the tribe's health clinic and the mentor of Kee Redhorse.

Betty Mills—Longtime administrator of the tribe's health clinic.

Oleg and Anton—Kacey's captors. She doesn't know their last names but thinks they are Russian.

Chapter One

Kacey Doka felt the warm gush of liquid surge down her thighs as her water broke. She knew what it meant, knew she must alert the guards. After eight months of captivity, she would be the first to see what happened next.

She didn't know what frightened her more, the prospect of giving birth or what they would do to her when she was finished.

"Don't tell them," said her friend Marta, her eyes wide with terror. Marta Garcia was also nineteen and had been taken before Kacey. She was bigger around the middle, so all the girls trapped with Kacey in this dusty basement thought that Marta would go first.

"They are going to notice a baby," said Brenda Espinoza, who was two years younger, was well into her second trimester and no longer able to deny the child that moved within her.

Brenda was the third to arrive. In May, according to their floor calendar, three months after Kacey.

"And that you're no longer pregnant," Brenda
added. "How do you expect to hide that?"

She didn't. Kacey knew that she had no alternative but to alert the guards. She glanced to Maggie
Kesselman, the newest arrival here, just over a week
ago. Kacey felt so sorry for her. Maggie was the
youngest at only fourteen and still grappling through
tears and disbelief at what had happened to her.

"Call them," said Kacey.

Marta walked laboriously up the wooden steps
from the basement to the metal door that opened
exactly twice a day. Marta glanced back with wide,
troubled eyes and Kacey nodded. Marta knocked and
then retreated down the stairs. All the windows were
covered from the outside and barred from within, so
the only light was the single overhead bulb that never
went out and that now cast Marta's shadow before
her as she descended. Marta hurried along with a
heavy, rocking tread, gripping the banister for support, anxious to be back on the cold concrete floor
before that door swung open because they didn't like
them hanging by the door when it opened.

Kacey did not know where they were being kept.
But she did know that screaming for help brought

only the guards. Vicious, heartless guards who spoke in a thick foreign accent.

"They'll find us soon," said Kacey to the other three. "They'll come and rescue us."

She kept saying it, believing it until the others believed it, too. Their families, their tribe, the authorities were all searching. They'd come for them.

"If I don't come back, I'll send help. I promise."

Marta hugged her. Maggie started to cry again. Brenda stared at the floor with an unfocused gaze, her hands laced, locked and pressed to her mouth.

Kacey knew the guards did not like being disturbed between feedings. Whatever they were doing, interruptions resulted in blows.

The door banged open and two men descended the stairs with clubs. The girls screamed and fled to the corners of the large empty basement area. Only Kacey remained at the bottom of the stairs.

Their captors had provided them each with a blanket and mattress. They also had a sink and toilet behind a partition. The toilet smelled of bleach and soap, both provided, but the basement held the musty scent of wool, dirt and decay. An appearance of a new mattress always signaled the imminent arrival of a new girl. Yesterday, the fifth mattress had appeared. To date, four had entered through that metal door and none had left. Kacey was about to leave their prison.

Would they bring her to a hospital to deliver her baby? No, of course they couldn't do that because she could speak to any of the medical staff and alert them that she was a prisoner.

"What is dis? Why you are knocking?" The one they called Oleg spoke to the group. His English was best but still difficult for them to understand.

The girls looked from one to the other, none willing to speak to Oleg because although his English was the best, his temper was the worst. Kacey's insides seemed to have a will of their own and began squeezing so hard that she cried out.

"Her water broke," said Marta, pointing to the wet spot on the concrete floor.

Oleg turned his pale blue eyes on Kacey. Then he glanced to the large pool of water darkening the concrete. He motioned his head toward Kacey, and the second man, Anton, stepped forward and captured Kacey by the arm, hurrying her toward the stairs.

She glanced over her shoulder to see the girls coming together in the center of the room, huddling tight as they stared after her. Oleg grasped her opposite arm and she was thrust up the stairs before them and through the prison door.

On the floor above the basement, she saw an office with tight dark carpeting and three desks with computers and phones under harsh fluorescent lighting. A television had been mounted on the wall, and a mini fridge sat beneath it with a half-full coffeepot resting on the top. The shape of the room and the two doorways made Kacey think she was in a large house. The normalcy of the layout clashed with the terror below her feet where the others huddled in near darkness.

The windows furnished views of a busy road where cars buzzed past trying to make the light. Beyond that squatted a strip mall, housing a Chinese restaurant, nail salon and pet grooming. The sunlight seemed especially bright and she used her hand as a visor.

"Call the boss," said Oleg.

Anton released her to move to the phone. The third guard, whom she had never seen, watched her intently as her eyes moved from Anton to the door and then to his face to see the wicked smile challenging her to go for it.

Kacey wrapped her arms around her squeezing stomach and clenched her teeth. Anton lowered the phone.

"The boss said he'll call the doc."

Oleg thrust her into one of the office chairs. Kacey's eyes went from the computer to the phone as she calculated her chances of using either. The big unfamiliar guard stalked forward and sat on the edge of the desk. Then he folded his arms across his wide chest. He looked so smug and superior that instead of feeling defeat, Kacey felt rage.

"Not there," said Anton. "She'll bleed all over everything. Take her to the exam room."

She was lifted by the upper arms with such force she momentarily left the floor. Kacey soon found herself in a small windowless room dominated by a short black examination table with two metal gizmos that reminded her of small riding stirrups. Her flesh began to crawl.

The pain ripped across her back and she doubled over.

"It hurt?" asked Oleg.

She nodded, blowing out a breath as sweat beaded on her forehead.

"Good. That mean baby is coming."

The door closed but not before she heard Anton ask Oleg, "What about her?"

Oleg's answer was not in English, but Anton's reply was.

"Dump her or sell her?" asked Anton.

She could not understand the reply but did not need to. She had her answer. After the baby was born, she would be sold or killed.

Kacey held her throbbing middle. She knew the child she carried was not hers. But somehow it did not matter. She loved it and would protect it. That meant staying alive.

She pounded on the door. "I need to use the toilet."

"Use the sink in there."

"I can't climb up on that sink!"

The door opened and Anton entered. He took her arm and hauled her up another flight of stairs to a very nice, clean bathroom with a claw-foot tub, white shower curtain, shampoo, conditioner, soap and clean towels. She scowled at the bounty as the anger built inside like lava. She and her friends had one bar of soap among all of them, worked down to a thin wafer. Meanwhile the guards had this. She glanced from the toilet to the small window.

"So go," said Anton.

He wanted to watch? Fine. She drew up the sheath dress they had provided and sat. After several minutes, he urged her to hurry.

"I'm not done."

"You better not have that kid in that toilet."

She had her weapon. Kacey closed her eyes and pushed, crying out. She peered at her captor. He was glancing back toward the hall.

Kacey cried louder.

"Oleg! Get up here." He stepped out of the door and vanished.

Kacey had the door shut and the bolt thrown in a moment. Anton pounded on the door as Kacey opened the window and scrambled out onto a flat roof overhanging the first floor. She ran to the edge and glanced to the lawn. It seemed a long way down. Then she turned back toward the house. How long did she have?

She threw one of her princess slippers off the roof. Then she threw the other one. The roof coating was so hot, it burned her feet. Kacey ran along the roof to the other side of the house, where she found a half-open window. She could see Oleg and the third man rush down the hall toward the bathroom.

Kacey was sliding the window open the rest of the way when she heard a crash. The bathroom door, she thought. Kacey slipped inside the house and down the stairs to the first floor as the men shouted from the bathroom. She hurried through the office and to the entrance hall. There on the stand beside a hat rack were three sets of car keys. She grabbed all three and was turning toward the basement door to release her friends when she saw Oleg through the dining room window as he passed by on the outside of the house. How had he got off the roof so fast?

They made eye contact and he shouted to the others,

breaking into a run. She glanced to the locked basement door. If she went that way, he'd have her.

Kacey made her decision and charged out the front door. She descended the porch stairs, hitting the unlock button on one of the car fobs. A car beeped. But that one was trapped behind the others. She tried again, reaching the drive as Oleg made it to the walkway.

The next car was the one she wanted. It looked new and fast. More important, it was closest to the road. She dived into the car as Oleg pounded both open hands on the hood, denting the metal.

She pressed the lock on the fob as his hand slipped onto the latch and tugged. Kacey looked for a key, but there was none. Just a button beside the steering wheel that said START. She pushed it and the engine turned over. There was no gearshift, just a knob. She rotated it to R as Oleg shattered the driver's-side window with his fist.

"I rip dat baby from your belly!" he bellowed.

His hand extended toward her, his fingers forming a claw. Kacey screamed and threw herself sideways across the console. Then she jammed her foot down on the gas. The car sailed backward down the drive, over the curb, hitting something that flew over the roof before she righted herself. She could barely reach the pedals because the seat was so far back, but she managed to get the car into Drive and turn the wheel so the tires were back on pavement as she raced away. She saw Anton running after her in the street. She thrust her arm out the open space where the window had been and extended her middle finger, giving him a gesture of farewell.

She had all their keys and she knew where they were keeping her friends. All she had to do was get to the police and tell them what had happened.

But Marta told her that she had heard Oleg say the police were on their payroll and that they knew about the house and did nothing. Not the police, then. Her tribe—tribal police. She had to get home to Turquoise Canyon.

Where was she? Sweat beaded on her forehead and her stomach muscles cramped. She slowed as she made a turn onto a strange road. The landscape was familiar. She looked around and then into the rearview at the way she had come. She knew they hadn't taken her far from home because of the amount of time she had ridden in the back of the van. Soon she had herself oriented.

She was in Darabee, Arizona. And everyone in her tribe knew that Darabee was the police force who had set the stage for the Lilac Shooter to be assassinated right in the station. The investigations were ongoing. The police chief had been replaced, but she believed what Marta had told her. This police force could be on the Russians' payroll, so she was not going there under any circumstances. Kacey was halfway to her home in Turquoise Canyon when she realized that this would be the first place they would look.

Her mother couldn't protect her, assuming she was even there. And going there would only put her brothers and sisters in danger. Her best friend, Marta, was still a captive. Kacey needed to get the girls out of there before they did something terrible to them all.

The tribal police, she trusted them. They could find the house. She drove to Piñon Forks, past the activity at the river, construction mostly, with dump trucks, bulldozers and backhoes. She ignored them as she drove to tribal headquarters. The parking lot was eerily empty. There were no police cars and no tribal vehicles. She drew up to the fire lane in front of the station, peering at the dark empty building.

Something was very wrong.

She craned her neck. Why were there no pickup trucks on the road? She had passed no one and seen not one soul since arriving on the rez. The town looked deserted. Where was everyone?

A car appeared in her rearview and she jumped. Was it Oleg?

The man who stepped out of the vehicle was white and wearing some sort of uniform. Her heart hammered as she considered fleeing before he reached her. But she needed information.

He approached from the driver's side. Kacey prepared to shift her foot from brake to gas. He stood before her window. She meant to lower it only a crack, but the window was gone, leaving her vulnerable. Her heart pounded in her throat.

"You looking for tribal headquarters?" he asked.

"Yes." Her voice sounded strange to her ears. Barely a squeak.

"They moved," he said.

What? Why? That didn't make any sense at all. "Where?" Her voice was all air and very little sound.

He cocked his head and gave her an odd stare as if she should know this.

"Up to Turquoise Ridge." He glanced at her distended belly. "Oh! Clinic is up there, too. They're in trailers, one beside the other. Can't miss it. You need me to drive you?"

"No. Thanks." She did not wait for a reply before accelerating away.

They'd moved? Why would tribal government ever leave their main community for the rough mining settlement of Turquoise Ridge?

The women's health clinic was right next to the

police station, looking just as deserted. But she couldn't go to the clinic, even if it were open, because the Russians would probably look for her there, because someone there had done this to her. She and the other girls had compared memories. They had all been to the tribal health-care facility shortly before capture. But what had happened there was a yawning blank, for her visits and theirs. Why couldn't they remember?

She had to get word to tribal police.

It was several minutes before Kacey became aware of her surroundings again. She was already in the tribal community of Koun'nde and heading for Turquoise Ridge. She should turn around.

And go where?

Where could she go where she would be safe and where they could not find her? Somewhere she could find help for her friends but not endanger her sisters and brothers?

And then she knew. She would go to him, the boy who had promised to go away with her and instead left her behind. Kacey knew he was scheduled to come home from Afghanistan. His brother Ty had told her so and that he was changed. He had been discharged after something that had happened over there. Ty said that Colt had been captured with comrades in an insurgent attack and then recovered.

Afterward Colt had spoken to Ty from Maryland and said he wasn't ready to come home. Ty talked him into coming back anyway. Colt agreed but only if he could live up in the family's claim off Dead Horse Road beyond the community of Turquoise Ridge.

Ty had told her Colt wanted to see her after he got his act together. But she'd been taken before he came home. She knew Colt's plan had been to make over an old cabin. Colt had shown it to her once. She knew where it was. It was a good place to hide, and if Colt was there, he could help her rescue her friends.

What she didn't know was if she had the physical strength to reach it. Her middle began to squeeze again and she bucked back in the seat, swerving dangerously. She had to reach him before her body forced her to stop, before the men pursuing her captured her again.

I rip dat baby from your belly.

She shivered at the memory of Oleg's words. The tears she had held for months now poured down her cheeks, blurring her vision. But she ignored the tears and pain in her middle and the ache in her heart as she pressed down on the gas.

Time had become the enemy.

COLT REDHORSE HEARD the screeching of brakes and the slide of tires on gravel as someone made the turn leading to his cabin way too fast. His brother Ty was known to drive like that in his youth, trying out the various cars he was improving. But lately he always approached Colt's retreat slowly and with proper notice. Often he sent his dog, Hemi, in first as envoy.

So it wasn't Ty.

Colt collected his rifle. The pistol was always on his hip or beside his head on those few occasions when he slept. He didn't sleep much. Too many ways for his enemies to reach him in dreams.

He moved between the trunks of the trees quickly and without much sound. Whoever it was would not hear him coming. He was like death itself—silent and without mercy.

Since he'd returned from Afghanistan, Colt's emotions boiled down to only two—fear and fury. Right now, it was just fury. No one came up here uninvited. His brother Jake had tried more than once. Colt hadn't shot at him, but it had been hard hiding while Jake violated his personal space. The mining cabin belonged to all of them, as did the claim. But the way he figured it, it was his by occupation and because he just couldn't stand to be around anyone yet. His skin itched like that of a junkie coming down from a high. He checked to see if a bug was crawling up his arm and saw only smooth brown skin.

He wasn't back in Afghanistan anymore, he told himself. He was home. This was Apache land. Safe land. This settlement lay tight against the turquoise-bearing ridge from which the town got its name.

Turquoise Ridge, the most remote of the three settlements on the Turquoise Canyon Reservation. Most folks here were miners. Living up on the ridge required a person to tote water and live without electricity or plumbing. Other than the miners, there were a few recluses, like him, he supposed. His closest neighbor was a Vietnam vet, former army, who went off the rez hoping to be a code talker like the Navajo and came home as crazy as Colt felt he himself was rapidly becoming. Randy Hooee hung tinfoil around his cabin to keep the CIA from listening to the thoughts in his head. As far as Colt could tell, it seemed to be working.

Colt's breathing slowed and his skin now only buzzed with adrenaline, not the flesh-crawling fear that threatened daily to have him hanging out bits of tinfoil, as well.

He had a purpose. Find the identity of the intruder.

He resumed his operation, moving close enough to see the road. The car was black and unfamiliar. A sedan, dust-covered with a dented hood. Parked at an odd angle and stationary now as the dust continued to settle back to earth. The tinted windshield showed him nothing. His eyes narrowed.

Why didn't they all just leave him alone?

The door opened and a hand appeared on the top of the driver's-side window. Small, slim and gripping hard as if the driver had to haul himself out of the car. Colt lifted the rifle, using the scope to aim at where he knew the center of the driver's torso would be in just a moment. Should he kill the bastard or just shoot out the windshield beside his head? He shifted between his two targets. This or that? That or this? A smile twisted his lips. He'd learned a lot from the US Marines but even more from the insurgents who had held him for three days.

And then the target's head popped up above the door frame like a fox leaving its den. Colt's hands went numb and he dropped his rifle.

It had been eighteen months, but he knew he would never forget that face. That was his former girlfriend, Kacey Doka. She'd tried to convince him not to join up after he graduated. Not to leave her behind. He had explained that if she wanted to get off the rez, this was their way. He hadn't wanted to go because he loved it here, couldn't imagine living anywhere else. But Kacey could and he loved her enough to try to give her what she wanted. It had cost him, deeply.

He had planned to give the signing bonus and his pay to her, but she wouldn't take it. She wanted them to go together, but he had committed himself. How had he messed that up so badly? She had not answered his letters. When he'd finally made it back home on a psych discharge, her home was the only place he'd stopped before coming here. Kacey had left, her mother said, months ago. She hadn't been back, wasn't expected back. But she sure was back now.

Kacey glanced up the hill toward his position, the sunlight highlighting her black hair blue. Colt flinched. Had she heard him drop his rifle? He watched her glance back the way she had come. From here, he could not see much of the road because of the trees. But she would have a clear view.

What was she doing here after all this time? He'd been home for months. Had Ty called her? That thought made his stomach flip. The only thing worse than being a walking basket case was having Kacey Doka know about it.

"Colt?" she called to him.

He pressed his back to the flaking bark of the ponderosa pine and squeezed his eyes shut.

Go away, Kacey. Please.

"Colt, it's Kacey!" She was shouting now. Judging from the sound, she was cupping her hands to her mouth to amplify her voice. "I need to see you."

No, you don't. Not like this.

Ty had sent her. Damn his meddling older brother. Colt had told him he didn't want to see anyone. That he wasn't ready. Had Ty given up hope that he was improving? But he was. He made it through more than one day without a panic attack. But the nights were very long. He knew his lack of sleep wasn't helping. But he wouldn't take anything that Ty had offered.

"I'm in trouble, Colt. Please, please answer me."

Trouble?

Colt's eyes opened as he pushed himself off the tree. What kind of trouble could she be in?

Was this a trick?

Despite her mother's neglect, Kacey had done well in school, missing only when her mom took off, leaving Kacey to take care of her siblings. Ty told him that Kacey had been accepted at Phoenix University and planned to use her Big Money for as long as it lasted. Big Money was what they called the allotment of the tribe's revenue distributed annually, but kept in trust for members under eighteen. The distributions often went for vehicles, something big and flashy. Colt noticed that there never was another new truck after that first one. He knew thirty-year-olds still driving that Big Money truck. So he had not spent his on a vehicle. Instead he kept his for them, him and Kacey. He figured his pay, his bonus and Big Money could get them a house right here on the rez.

He was certain that if he could get them their own place and provide her a real home, she would change her mind about leaving. To do that, he'd enlisted in the Marines. That was when she'd ended it between them. When Ty told him she'd gone, Colt had been expecting it.

Had she used her Big Money to run away?

She'd loved him once. He knew that. And he had loved her, which was why he wasn't going to let her see him now. It would kill those feelings she'd held as surely as a snake crushes a baby bunny.

But he could see her. He'd give himself that at least. Just for a minute and then he'd go.

"I'm coming up there. Don't you shoot me, Colt Redhorse, or so help me, I will tell your mother."

His mother liked Kacey and she was worried about him. Ty had said so. And his mother wasn't well. Why didn't Ty tell him that Kacey was back? He could have used a little warning to prepare.

He heard the crunch of her footsteps as she crossed the gravel on the road. Her tread was slow and heavy.

And she gave a cry as if she was in pain. Colt popped his head around the trunk of the tree. What he saw made his jaw drop.

Was Kacey pregnant?

She was! Very, very pregnant and she was holding her swollen belly as her face twisted into a mask of pain. His eyes widened. He'd seen that same expression on his mother's face when she went into labor with his little sister, Abbie. He'd only been six, but the fear made the memory stick.

Was Kacey in labor?

That was impossible. You'd have to be crazy to come up here to deliver a baby. He craned his neck to see her as she momentarily disappeared from view behind the trees. She was heading for the trail they had used to climb up to his family's cabin. She knew the way.

Kacey had been a part of his family, had spent more time living in his house than in hers. Not that he blamed her. But she'd go home when her sister Jackie or Winnie would come and tell her that their mom was gone again. Running drugs for the Wolf Posse, Ty said, taking her cut in either money or product.

Colt moved parallel to Kacey as she walked along the road toward the trail, catching flashes of Kacey between the tree trunks. She looked thin, despite her swollen belly, and pale as if she had not been in the sun in months. Her gait was a scurry that combined the side-to-side rocking motion of a woman far along in her pregnancy with a girl in a hurry. She held both hands under her belly. Why did she keep looking behind her?

Kacey stopped, hunched and turned toward the road. What could she see that made her eyes round and her mouth swing open like a gate? Kacey ran now. She ran to the woods and rock outcropping with a speed he would not have believed possible.

"They're here! Colt, do you hear me? They're going to take me again."

Again?

Oh no, they are not.

Colt didn't know who *they* were or why they were after Kacey. What he did know was that they wouldn't succeed in reaching her. He had the high ground, a rifle with extra rounds and the will to kill anyone who threatened Kacey. He might be a mental mess, but he remembered what it felt like to be in love with her. But now that memory only made his chest ache and his breathing hitch. Whatever part of him that understood how to love a woman had died back there in Afghanistan. But that didn't mean he wouldn't protect her. He would, with his life.

Colt moved to a position that gave him a good

vantage of her car and waited as the second vehicle approached. Colt lifted the rifle, pressing the familiar stock to his cheek and closing his left eye. The crosshairs fixed on the gray sedan.

He felt centered, calm, relaxed.

The first shot sent a bullet at the driver's side of the windshield. The glass should have shattered into tiny cubes but instead remained intact. The second shot went to the passenger's side. If there was a passenger behind the windshield, he should now have a bullet in his head, but instead the glass showed only a tiny nick. Colt was using .38 long-range ammunition. That windshield should be compromised. But it wasn't and he knew why. The glass was reinforced.

"Bulletproof," he muttered.

He had not seen that since Afghanistan. This was a very expensive vehicle. From within the luxury auto, someone shifted the sedan's gears and the car reversed direction with a spray of gravel.

Colt marched down the hill. When he reached the road, the car was turning around. He got two shots into the side of the vehicle with nothing but damage to the paint. He missed the shot at the rear tire. The next shot pinged off the rear window of the retreating sedan. Who the heck was after her?

Whoever it was, they had money—lots of money.

He put a hole in the license for no reason except

as a final farewell and a good riddance. If they came back, he'd use a hand grenade on their asses.

Colt turned to the woods, where Kacey now stood beside the outcropping of rock she had used for cover. She bent forward at the hips, clutching her belly with one hand and the boulder with the other, eyes pinched shut. Colt had a sickening feeling that while he had been up here brooding over Kacey's departure and collecting the bits and pieces of his mind, Kacey had been in real trouble. He was equally afraid she was going to have that baby right here and right now.

Chapter Two

"They're gone," Colt said, his voice slightly deeper than she remembered. He was at her side in an instant, rifle slung over his shoulder. His long black hair hung straight and loose past his shoulders. She met his stare, seeing the familiar espresso color of his irises, just slightly lighter than his pupils. His skin was bronze from the sun and his brows were thicker than she recalled, balancing the rich brown of his eyes and the symmetrical nose that seemed small by contrast to his wide mouth and full lips. The cleft in his chin looked deeper and his face leaner. He'd lost weight but gained muscle, she realized, making his body look harder and more dangerous.

She was safe. For the first time in months and months, she was safe and she was home. The joy bubbled up inside. She threw her arms around his neck, kissing him full on the lips. The warm familiar scent of pine and warm male skin enveloped her.

He stiffened as their bodies met, his hands coming up to her shoulders, and for a moment she thought he would push her away. For another heartbeat, he hesitated and then he gathered her up and held her as his mouth took hers, deepening the kiss. She was home in his arms and everything would be—

He gripped her shoulders, increasing the tension as he pushed her to arm's length. He stared at her, panting and feral, like a mad dog. Then he pressed his hand over his mouth and wiped away her kiss. The pain in her stomach morphed from sorrow at his rejection to another contraction. She grimaced and groped behind her for the solid security of the rock, seating herself as the contraction gripped her.

He was not the boy she recalled, the one who kissed her and told her that he'd come back for her. That boy had been joyful and optimistic. But the man before her was taller, leaner and harder than Colt Redhorse. There was a wildness around the whites of his eyes that reminded her of a mustang the instant he feels the rope cinch around his neck. Colt's nostrils flared and he stepped back, his gaze sweeping down to her bare feet and then back up to her face.

She imagined what he must think, and the shame sent a guilty flush into her face, making it burn with heat. Kacey placed a hand on her distended belly and the other on the hollow below her cheekbone. Somehow in just over a year, everything had changed between them and they were strangers.

Beneath the skin, her muscles were contracting, sending pressure all the way around to her back. This one was worse. She hunched and groaned, squeezing her eyes shut.

"You shouldn't do that. I'm not… I can't."

She heard the blast of air as he forcefully exhaled.

"They'll come back for the baby."

Colt glanced down the road in the direction of their retreat.

"Should I bring you to the clinic?" he asked.

Her reply was a shout. "No!"

Colt flinched. "All right. Where, then? Your mom's?"

"They'll look for me there. My sisters and brothers, I don't want anything to happen to them." Finally the pressure in her back eased and she could straighten. That was when she noted that Colt had one arm around her. The other she gripped, squeezing with a force that matched the contraction. She released his arm and saw the white print of her hand disappear as the blood returned to his forearm.

How long would this go on? It had been over an hour already.

"How did you know where to find me?"

"Ty said you agreed to come home after your discharge if you could come here." She didn't mention the reason for his discharge. Had Ty told her that his kid brother had been a POW, rescued and returned stateside?

"So you came here looking for me?" Colt asked.

She lowered her gaze. "I didn't know what else to do."

He made a sound in his throat and then said, "I'm honored."

Kacey's mouth dropped open and her gaze flashed to him. Colt smiled down at her and for a moment everything was good again. He was here with her and she knew he would protect her.

She looked up at him, noting the unfamiliar breadth of his shoulders. His hair gleamed with good health. She reached up and fingered a strand, placing it on his chest and pressing it into place.

"They didn't make you cut it," she said. His hair still reached to his chest and she was so glad.

"Nope. Just made me wear it tied back and under my shirt or in a bun."

"A bun?" Imagining that made her smile. He smiled, too.

His wide mouth drew back to reveal white, even teeth. He'd had the chip in the front repaired and now she could not even remember which tooth he had damaged. His jaw was more prominent, as were his cheekbones.

"You're too skinny," she said.

He pressed his mouth closed, still smiling as he nodded. "That's what Ty says, too."

"You see him? How is he?"

Colt shook his head. "I don't talk to him."

Her brow wrinkled. "But you said—"

"He comes sometimes. He talks to me. I let him see me. But I don't speak to him. I don't speak to anyone."

Her frown deepened.

"But me?" she asked.

He blew out a breath through his nose. "I guess so."

"How long have you lived like this?"

"Since they released me."

"Released?"

Didn't she know? But she didn't. He could see it in the wide earnest expression that showed nothing but confusion. Well, he sure wasn't going to tell her.

His lips went tight. He led her down to the car. "Let's get you out of here."

She took a few steps and then stopped. "I can't go to one of the settlements or the police."

"Why?"

"They're looking for me. They'll take me again."

His eyes shifted and one hand went to the strap of his rifle. "Who?"

"Those two and I don't know who else. I heard more of them. But I've only ever seen Oleg and Anton. Oh, and one other guy. I don't know his name."

"Oleg?"

"Russians."

He looked back toward the road. "They have an armored car." He swung the rifle before him, lifting it to his shoulder. "Plug your ears," he said.

She did and he took a shot. The bullet punched a hole in the rear door of the car she had stolen.

"That one isn't armored." He swung the rifle so the strap held it behind his back. "Okay. Let's go farther up into the ridge. There's a second cabin."

"Anyone know that?"

"Ty."

"Let's go." She allowed him to help her to the car and flushed as he pulled the safety belt over her distended belly and clipped it in place. She sank into the seat, closing her eyes.

"How long did they have you?" he asked.

She turned to him, opening her eyes. "Since February."

"February!" He straightened, his brow sweeping down over his dark eyes. That was eight months.

"Yeah."

"Everyone said you ran away."

"I didn't." She reached and gripped his hand. "Colt, there are more of us. More like me and they're all from Turquoise Canyon."

Now he was staring down the road where they had gone. "I could call Jake. Maybe he could pick them up."

"You have a phone?" she asked.

He shook his head.

"They'll kill Jake." The next contraction built across her middle.

He gripped her door frame and glanced down the empty road. "But you said there were others."

Her eyes widened. "Yes. Three others. They have Marta Garcia. She was in my class in high school. They took her before me. And Brenda Espinoza. She's five months pregnant. And Maggie Kesselman. They're all like me." She motioned to her belly. "Marta's due any day."

"What will happen to them now that you escaped?"

A cold shot of terror ripped through her. "I don't know." But the possibilities terrified her.

"We have to tell Jake," said Colt.

His brother was the newest hire on the tribal police force and she knew he could be trusted.

"I think so."

Her back cramped. "Oof!" she said and clutched her middle.

"We're getting you somewhere safe. But I need to find a woman to help you."

"No. Anyone who sees this baby is in danger. Colt, I wish I could have thought of a way by myself. But I'm scared. I need your help."

"But I've never—"

"Neither have I."

He shook his head and she saw something she had not seen before in him: fear.

"Colt Redhorse, you left me once. Don't you dare do that again."

She'd told him not to go. She'd felt something terrible would happen to him. As it turned out, something terrible had happened to both of them.

"I promised to come back."

"You didn't."

"I did. But you were gone."

She glowered at him.

"I'll get you somewhere safe, Kacey. I promise."

Kacey sighed. The air here was so sweet and clean. She thought of the musty basement where she'd been kept for months and shuddered.

"So, call Jake. All right?" he asked.

She nodded.

He rounded the hood at a run. A moment later,

they were in motion on the rough road, heading back toward the center of Turquoise Ridge.

COLT HEADED FOR David SaVala's claim. It was close and David could be trusted to deliver a message to Ty. Ty could get to Jake. Then Colt was going to take Kacey to his cabin and help her bring this baby into the world. Colt planned on keeping this car hidden but close in case he needed to get Kacey to a hospital. With luck, Ty would be here soon.

Colt had three older brothers and his younger sister. The oldest brother was Kee, newly board certified as a doctor. Colt wished he could bring Kacey to him, but she would not go near the clinic. He planned to find out why. His next oldest brother was Ty, who, unlike Colt, had made it through his service in the US Marines to be honorably discharged. His tales of the service had convinced Colt to join.

But Ty had not chosen to enlist. He had signed to avoid federal prosecution after he and their father were arrested for armed robbery. Ty had already been in the Wolf Posse, the tribe's gang. The tribal leadership felt he needed discipline, so a deal was struck. Charges dropped if Ty enlisted. His father had previous arrests, so the tribe allowed federal prosecution. Now Ty lived between the gang who had claimed him and the family that couldn't keep him from choosing that life. Ty had often said it was easier to leave the military than a gang.

Finally there was Jake, the newest member of the Turquoise Tribal Police and six years Colt's senior. Jake had looked after him when their father went to prison. Colt had been lucky. He'd sort of had three fathers.

"Ty lives in Koun'nde. He has a phone. If I can get SaVala to lend me his phone, we can take it far enough to get service and call Ty and Jake. Then I can call Kee and ask him to come deliver this baby."

She had her eyes closed again and was blowing through pursed lips. Sweat beaded on his brow.

"Kacey?" he whispered.

She turned her head to look at him, her cheeks puffing out and in as she blew.

"They won't get you," he promised.

Her head dropped to the headrest. He knew she was already nineteen, but she still looked like the girl he'd first loved, still loved. Why had he left her? She'd been right about everything. Something terrible had happened to him and to her. He'd been so sure that the Marines would be a shortcut to what she wanted, with money to provide the life away from her mother and the shadow of his father. He'd been trying to prove he was strong like his brother Ty and smart like Kee and good like Jake. But he wasn't any of those things. He was a fragile wreckage of a man who couldn't even talk to people since…well, since everything that had happened over there.

He hadn't had the chance to be a hero. He'd just been taken like a sheep from a pasture to the butcher truck. Fate had made him the last lamb in line.

He pressed the web of his hand between his thumb and index finger to his forehead, trying to ease the pounding. He was in a car again and there was not enough air. He released his head to grip the wheel, bracing for the blast, waiting for it.

This time he'd be ready.

Colt was not going back there now. Kacey needed him. He was here on Turquoise Canyon and he had to stay focused. But he knew he wasn't keeping the panic attack away. He was only postponing it. The doc at Walter Reed in Maryland said he needed counseling and put him on the list. With luck, it would be decades before they would get to his name, because he wasn't talking about that with anyone ever. No one who wasn't held by insurgents could possibly understand.

His gaze flicked to Kacey, who sat with her head dropped back on the headrest but turned toward him. She smiled at him, her face relaxed and her hands laced over her belly. Her dark hair was gathered in a loose braid that lay on her shoulder. Her once soft, round face had changed. Her deep brown eyes were still bright, but there were dark smudges beneath them. Her lips were full and pink, but her jaw and pointed chin seemed too prominent in her thin face. How much weight had she lost? Kacey had always been slender, but now she was skinny, way too skinny. How much had they given them to eat?

Not enough—clearly.

The rations that he'd been given during his captivity rose in his mind and he pushed the memory of that down. One sure way to be of no help to her was to think about that.

No one understood that the captivity wasn't as hard as the memories that just would not go away. It wasn't getting better with time. It was worse. Colt gripped the wheel. He hated cars, trucks, anything that rolled. No one in his family understood. They were worried, but they didn't get it. He could not think about it, but he was stuck somehow. Afraid all the time.

Kacey was now looking in the side mirror, watching for trouble. Perhaps she could understand, he realized. Because she'd been a captive, too. But then she'd also understand that he was the very last person capable of helping her. That was why he was leaving her with his brother. Any one of his brothers was a better choice than him.

The corner of his mouth twitched.

"Almost there," he said to himself as much as to her.

Chapter Three

Kacey's body relaxed. The contractions were not as strong now, fading as if taking a pause. How long did labor last? Hours? Days? She didn't know. Her mother just went to the clinic and came home the next day with a brother or sister. Kacey assumed that by tomorrow at this time, she would have a baby. But exactly what happened in the meantime was vague.

She'd learned about childbirth in high-school health class. At the time, the lesson seemed theoretical. The abstract phases of birth just one more thing to be memorized and spit back on a quiz. Stage I—Early Labor. Stage II—Active Labor. Stage III—hand the baby to a nurse and take a nap.

Colt pulled off the road and up a short turnoff that was composed of two ruts in the yellow grass. A cabin came into view against the ridge, sitting up on concrete blocks. The step before the front door was clearly slag rock from a turquoise vein. She was Turquoise Canyon Apache, so she recognized what base rock surrounded a vein of the precious blue stone.

Colt barely had the car in Park before throwing himself against the driver's-side door in his hurry to be out of the cab. He scrambled out onto all fours. It took him a moment to right himself before he straightened and returned to the car.

"Colt?"

He was sweating as if he'd run from his claim to this one. He peered in at her through the open door.

"Call him," he whispered.

Kacey opened her door and swung her legs out, bare feet touching the long yellow grass as she inched forward on the seat. Colt retrieved his rifle and then rounded the car to stand beside her door.

She called a greeting. They were met first by a skinny white dog. The muck on his shoulder showed he'd been rolling in something, and the stench said it was something dead.

The claim holder arrived shortly afterward, dressed in coveralls coated with a fine white layer of rock dust. All claims belonged to the tribe, but families worked them and passed them along. Her family's claim was worked by others, leased for a period of five years at a time.

David SaVala tried to shake Colt's hand, but Colt chose to place his hand on the shoulder strap of his rifle. David greeted her instead, peering at her from beside Colt, but his smile was gone.

"Good to see you two back together."

She smiled and nodded. That seemed easier than explaining.

David took another step toward her, moving beyond the open car door, and his step faltered.

"Oh." He glanced from her swollen belly to Colt. "Oh, I see. Congratulations, you two."

Kacey used the door and the frame to heave herself up. Colt rubbed his neck but said nothing. He backed toward the woods, but Kacey gripped his arm to prevent his escape.

She told David what they needed and he retreated to his cabin with his dog for the phone and handed it off to her with the pass code and instructions on where she would first find a signal. The distance and her condition required another car ride. They headed out with the dog trotting with them as far as the road. Colt was shaking by the time they reached the high point of Dead Elk Dip and the place that allowed a weak cell phone signal.

"What's wrong?" she asked.

"Don't drive anymore."

"Claustrophobic?" she asked. This was new. Ty had told her of Colt's capture but had been short on details. She just now understood what helping her was costing him. Was it leaving his claim that upset him or the driving?

His skin was pale. He retrieved David's phone. Colt placed the call and gripped his hair in one fist as he waited for the phone to connect.

Kacey heard a male voice issue a greeting.

Colt squeezed his eyes shut. His fist tightened in his hair.

"Who's this?" came the voice on the other end of the line.

His jaw clamped shut and he thrust the phone at her.

"Hello?" she replied.

"This is Redhorse." She recognized the voice of Officer Jake Redhorse, one of Colt's older brothers. Kacey identified herself and relayed the high points. Escape. The stolen car. The gun battle. Her condition and the location of the missing girls.

"You're with Colt?" Disbelief resonated in his voice.

"Yes. He's the one who called you."

There was a moment's pause.

"Where are the girls?"

"I don't know exactly. I just drove until I figured out where I was."

"I need the exact address," said Jake. "And if it's in Darabee, I need to notify their police department."

"No. They might be connected. Like they were with that assassination in their station. Karl Hooke and the Lilac Mine Mass Shooter," said Kacey.

"How do you know that?"

"Marta Garcia overheard our captors say so before I got there." Kacey knew that the Darabee police were being investigated by the federal and state government for corruption. Several of the force had been suspended and charges filed.

"Can I speak to Colt?" Jake asked.

She relayed the request and was met with a firm shake of his head.

"He says no."

"I'm calling my chief for instructions and en route to you. Head toward Turquoise Ridge. Okay?"

"Yes. I understand."

"I'll need you to identify the house, Kacey. Can you do that?"

That meant going back. She gripped her free hand to her throat. "I'm in labor and those killers are still out there."

"So are your friends," Redhorse reminded her.

That hit her harder than the contractions. Colt shook his head. Clearly he did not want her to go back.

She had promised them that she'd send help. "Yes. I'll go."

Jake told her to tell Colt what to expect and ended the call.

Now Kacey's heart was pounding. "He said the FBI is coming for that car."

Colt scowled.

She imagined they could find something in there, fingerprints at least. A clear image of Oleg smashing his hands on the hood of the car came to her. She glanced at the twin dents there as a shot of panic made her ears ring.

"Where? From Phoenix?"

"No. Your brother said that they have FBI in Piñon Forks since the explosion. Colt, what happened? What explosion? What is he talking about?"

"You must have passed through Piñon Forks on the way here. Didn't you see it?"

"I saw construction vehicles. The station was abandoned. Some man in a uniform told me that tribal headquarters had moved to Turquoise Ridge. But I took off before he told me why."

"Everyone has moved to Turquoise Ridge. They're in FEMA trailers or reclaiming their mining cabins."

"Why?"

"Come on. Let's get David's phone back to him."

En route, he told her everything, and the happenings were tragic. Some eco-extremists organization had blown up Skeleton Cliff Dam in hopes of compromising the Phoenix electrical grid. The dam was upriver from their reservation. Destroying the dam meant flooding their biggest community, Piñon Forks.

Apparently, an explosives expert from the FBI had managed to make a temporary barrier on their river by demolishing a huge section of the canyon ridge. Her actions had saved everyone there. But the rubble dam was failing. Evacuations were necessary.

She thought back to her wild race through town early this morning.

"I didn't even look at the canyon rim," she admitted. Her focus had been internal, on her own body, and external to the men she knew would come for her. "Have you seen it?"

He shook his head. "Haven't been off this claim since I got home. Until today. Heard about it from Ty. Only happened a couple weeks ago. Let's see. Third week in September, so nearly three weeks ago now."

He put his hand on the door latch and froze. He wiped a hand across his upper lip.

"I'll drive," she said.

"You're in labor."

"I know. Let me." She held her hand out for the fob.

He hesitated, then gave it to her and stepped aside.

"I'm sorry," he whispered.

She jostled herself awkwardly down into the seat

and waited as he rounded the hood and then paused at the passenger side. She lowered the window. "Get in."

"I can't."

"Colt, please."

"I'll run to David's place. Through the woods. Be there before you get there."

"What if they're waiting on the road?"

Colt climbed in, his expression grim. He folded his arms over his chest as if he were freezing. She didn't even suggest the seat belt as she put them in motion. She headed back to David SaVala's claim. On arrival, she tooted the horn, afraid if she got out, Colt would run. David's dog was still covered in something, and David appeared shortly afterward. He approached her window and she returned the phone. The dog jumped up and placed her front paws on the door, giving Kacey a stomach-turning whiff of dead animal.

"Get down," he said, pushing the dog off. "Sorry. She found a dead deer and keeps getting after it."

Kacey smiled and exhaled, trying to rid her nostrils of the stench.

The miner leaned down to look through the cab to Colt.

"Good to see you out, Colt," said David. "Been worried."

Colt nodded but said nothing. Why wouldn't he speak to anyone?

David glanced at Kacey, who gave him a shrug.

"My dad was in Vietnam," said David. "Still jumps at every truck that backfires. It changes you, I guess." He pushed himself off the car, straightened and forced a tight smile.

"Thank you for the use of the phone," she said.

"Sure." He scraped his knuckles over the stubble on his jaw. "Well, stop by anytime. Love company. Don't get much, though."

They were off a moment later with David waving after them despite the dust they kicked up. The rainy season had come and gone. They were back to hot, dry days and cold, clear nights.

Jake met them en route with three other vehicles. Colt drew his pistol and flicked the safety off.

Kacey was suffering from the end of another contraction, so she spoke through gritted teeth as she clutched the wheel. "Don't shoot your brother."

He nodded and holstered his weapon before leaving the vehicle. Kacey watched as he greeted Jake with a nod. Kacey knew the two men who exited the next vehicle. The first was Detective Jack Bear Den. No mistaking him because he was the biggest man she knew. From the opposite side of the SUV came tribal police chief Wallace Tinnin. He was limping, as if he'd injured his foot. The chief had come to speak to her high-school class her senior year. It had been the January awards assembly and he had shaken her hand when she made the honor roll. Had that only been ten months ago? Yes, she realized. Just months before she had been taken.

The next two cars were black sedans with tinted windows. FBI, she guessed. She didn't recognize the man or woman who exited the first vehicle but was surprised to see they both appeared to be Native American.

From the next sedan came two white men with short military-style haircuts and dark glasses. They had the same stony expressions as the Secret Service men who guarded the president.

Jake approached her door and she leaned out the broken window.

"We're going to transfer you to Detective Bear Den's unit, Kacey. That be all right?"

She nodded and he opened the door.

Colt was already speeding away from the vehicle.

Jake helped Kacey rise and then looked across the hood to Colt.

"Good to see you, brother," he said.

Colt looked away.

Jake glanced to her and she shook her head. She did not understand any better than he did why Colt would not speak.

"Did he talk to you?" Jake said, his voice low.

She nodded.

Jake released a sigh and escorted her toward the SUV. On her way, they paused for introductions. The man was FBI field agent Lieutenant Luke Forrest of the Black Mountain Apache tribe. The woman was FBI explosives expert Sophia Rivas, also of the Black Mountain Apache people.

"Are you the one who saved our town?" asked Kacey.

"Well, I had some help." She glanced at Bear Den, and Kacey sensed their relationship might be more than professional. "But I set the charges."

"Colt says you stopped the river from destroying Piñon Forks."

"That's true. Why don't you sit with me? I have a few questions."

Kacey cast a look at Colt. She was not leaving him.

"We're riding with Bear Den and Colt's brother," she said.

"All right. I'll just come along. That be okay?"

Kacey glanced to Colt, who inclined his chin.

"All right."

The contractions were now just an irregular flurry of spasms across her belly and back.

She walked past the last two men, who scanned her from head to toe.

Once past them, she asked Sophia Rivas who they were.

"Our guys. They're taking possession of your vehicle."

"Evidence?" asked Kacey.

Rivas smiled and nodded. "We sure hope so."

Bear Den held the rear door of his SUV open for Kacey. She struggled to climb inside. She wished she had something better to wear than the ugly sheath of a dress they'd given her. But what was important was getting to her friends before something happened to them. Those men, Oleg and Anton, they couldn't fight against all these law-enforcement officers.

Could they?

Colt slipped in beside her and she gripped his hand, fingers laced. He gave her comfort and she hoped she did the same for him. Jake took the front seat. Rivas climbed into the opposite side, so Colt slid to the middle of the broad back seat, separating her from the FBI agent.

Jake Redhorse told them that the FBI had opted not to notify the Darabee police of their presence based on the information she had given Officer Redhorse. So they sailed through town and back toward the house she had fled only four hours earlier.

Her contractions were no longer increasing in strength or frequency and they interfered little on the ride back from the rez to Darabee. What was going on? she wondered.

Still, her body concerned her less than the tic Colt displayed beneath his eye and the way he repeatedly flexed and stretched his free hand like a beating heart. His breathing was irregular, as if he were in pain.

She answered all Rivas's questions as they rode back down the mountain and through the settlement of Turquoise Ridge. Bear Den asked a few questions as they covered the road between Turquoise Ridge and Koun'nde. Then Jake told them some things that she hadn't known.

A classmate of hers and Colt's, Zella Colelay, had delivered a baby girl on September 23, the Saturday before last. She'd left the infant in Jake Redhorse's truck and he was being granted temporary custody of the baby by the tribe.

"You're getting custody?" asked Kacey. She did not quite keep the disbelief from her voice. A single man wanting custody of a baby was unusual.

"Lori Morgan and I are back together now. She's agreed to be my wife."

Kacey blinked at this news. She knew that Jake and Lori had once been a couple. Rumors were that Lori had got into trouble and the teens had been encouraged to marry before the baby came. Colt had confirmed it and told her that the miscarriage had wrecked the relationship. Now it seemed a new baby had brought them back together again.

"Congratulations," said Kacey.

Jake grinned. "Thanks. Just got married." He lifted his left hand, showing the gleaming gold band. Jake looked to Colt. "I wanted you there, brother. Have you stand up with me."

Colt lifted his shoulders and shuddered.

"What about Zella?" asked Kacey. "What will happen to her?"

Bear Den took that one. "She's been relocated, faces charges for abandonment of the infant. But she's young, and with the circumstances, I doubt she'll receive more than community service."

"One more thing," said Jake. "The baby. It's white."

Kacey frowned and rested her hands on her belly. How could Zella deliver a white baby? Did he mean the baby was a mix of Apache and Caucasian or what some here called a mix-up? Was Zella like her and the rest of the captives? Had this happened to her but somehow she had evaded capture? "Does Zella have a boyfriend?"

"No. She told us she has never been with a boy."

Kacey gasped. Just like her, Marta and Maggie. She needed to speak to Zella. Kacey turned to Colt to tell him that Zella might be one of them and she noticed he was trembling.

Colt's eyes were darting about and his leg was bouncing like that of a junkie coming off a high. She pressed a hand to his knee.

"You okay?" she whispered.

He jumped at her touch and then clutched her hand so hard she winced. Colt had not even visited his family since his return from Afghanistan. Now he was surrounded by people.

"I need to get out of this car," he said. "We're trapped back here."

"Pull over," said Kacey.

Bear Den glanced back at them in his rearview mirror.

"What?" said Bear Den.

"We can't stop," said FBI agent Rivas.

Colt's gaze flashed to the closed door.

"The baby. Pull over," said Kacey.

He did and the line of cars behind them stopped, as well. The lead car drove a few yards on and then noticed the delay and also pulled over.

Kacey tried the handle and found it locked.

Bear Den was quick for a big man. He had her door open an instant later and Kacey slid sideways, legs out of the SUV. Colt bolted past her and ran a few feet. Then he stopped, facing them, panting. His complexion was gray and his eyes were wild.

"Colt?" said Jake, hands raised.

Colt had his hand on his pistol.

"Take your hand off the weapon. No one is going to hurt you."

"I have to go back," he said. His eyes were wild as he searched for escape.

"Colt. Kacey needs you," said Rivas.

Colt stared at her, his expression tortured. "I'm sorry. I thought I could…"

"It's all right, Colt. You don't have to go," Kacey assured him.

"Don't get in that Humvee, Kacey," he said, pointing at the SUV. "Don't go. They'll take you."

Kacey's blood iced. It was her greatest fear, to be taken again, by the Russians, the feds, the Darabee police. Her throat went so dry she couldn't even swallow and she wanted to go with him.

"Not a Humvee," said Bear Den, his words an aside to Tinnin.

"Colt," said Rivas. "You're scaring Kacey."

Kacey headed toward Colt. She needed to touch him. Bring him back and save herself from the terror now crawling over her skin like scorpions.

"Don't," said Bear Den, clasping her arm and holding her back.

Colt made a feral sound between a snarl and a roar as his eyes were pinned on the place Bear Den touched Kacey.

"Let go," said Kacey.

Bear Den's hand dropped away. Kacey continued forward to Colt as he drew his pistol, holding it down and at his side. Behind her, she heard handguns leaving their plastic holsters. When she reached Colt, she took his face in her hands and pressed her forehead to his.

"I'm here, Colt. You're safe. You're home."

His body relaxed and his breathing slowed. "Stay with me," he said.

"It'll be all right."

"Don't go with them."

"I have to. I promised them, my friends, that I would send help. I have to go. Can Jake take you home?"

He nodded. The pistol slid from his fingers, thudding to the ground.

"All right. Wait for me. I'll be right back."

It was what he had said to her before he shipped out for boot camp. *I'll be right back.* That had been nearly two years ago.

He shuddered and turned to Jake, who was already holding his brother's abandoned handgun. The two brothers walked back along the line of cars to

Jake's police unit, which had been driven by Chief Wallace Tinnin. Jake helped Colt into the rear seat and then shut him in. Colt's eyes darted about the closed compartment. What had happened to him? Kacey wondered. Jake hurried behind the wheel as Colt locked his fingers together behind his head and ducked like an airline passenger preparing for impact. The vehicle made a U-turn and sped away.

When Kacey returned to the vehicle, it was to find FBI field agent Luke Forrest in the passenger's seat, Jack Bear Den driving and Sophia Rivas holding open the rear door for her. Kacey felt alone and afraid. Her heart beat so hard that it hurt. But she thought of Marta's pretty thin face and her own promise.

She hoisted herself back into the rear seat. "Let's go."

Chapter Four

Colt felt so dizzy he thought he would pass out. When he finally lifted his head from his hands, it was to discover he no longer had a pistol in his holster and he was sitting belted into the rear seat of Jake's police unit like a criminal.

Call Ty, he wanted to say to Jake. But he couldn't manage to say the words aloud.

Ty had been to the cabin, and unlike with Jake, Colt had let Ty see him. He never spoke to Ty when he came, but it was good to hear Ty's voice and his words—until it wasn't and Colt had to step away into the forest again.

Jake didn't move to retrieve his phone as he drove away from Koun'nde. Colt released the restraining belt and slid to the far side of the rear seat so he could see more than the back of Jake's head.

"Let me out," said Colt. He'd said that aloud, he realized. Or he thought he had. Jake did not reply.

His brother did glance at him in the rearview mirror, brows lifted in surprise. Colt felt a cold trickle of dread shiver down his spine. "Will they bring Kacey back to me?"

Jake adjusted his grip on the wheel. His expression was stony as he clenched his jaw.

The grim look on Colt's brother's face made him feel sick. He needed to get out of this car.

"She's in labor. They'll bring her to a hospital or call in a midwife, like Lori."

He was talking about the woman Jake had dated in high school. Now his wife, Colt remembered. He looked back in the direction they had taken Kacey. This was better. She was with people who didn't collapse into the past every time they heard an engine. People who weren't afraid to go out in the world.

"You got her to safety, Colt. You did a good job."

Until he'd freaked out again. It was why he couldn't come off the ridge. Why he was such a bad choice to look out for Kacey. He knew it. Everyone knew it. Why didn't Kacey?

"It's good to see you, brother, and to hear your voice. We've been…" Jake's words trickled off.

Colt continued to look back at the empty road behind them. What if they were waiting back there for

Kacey? He spun in the rear seat and stared back the way they had come.

"They've got her. She has three units," said Jake, interpreting his movements.

Colt recalled the semiautomatic weapons Kacey said the Russians had used.

"Turn around," said Colt.

"What?"

"Go after them."

"Colt, we need to get you home to Turquoise Ridge. I called Kenshaw Little Falcon."

That was the tribe's shaman. He was also a licensed therapist and had two degrees. Psychology and philosophy, Colt recalled. Ty had been trying to get Colt to see him for months.

"No. I need to get Kacey."

"Maybe tomorrow."

Colt laced his fingers through the cage that divided the front and back seats and shook the metal barrier. "Now."

Jake glanced at him in the rearview. "You drew your gun, Colt. On me and on federal agents. Do you even remember that?"

He didn't.

"You're lucky you're not in federal custody right now or dead. Now I owe Tinnin for the rest of my life for letting me take you home. We had to use the

sovereignty of our tribe to get Agent Forrest to release custody. But you can't see Kacey and you can't
leave the reservation. Got it?"

Colt stared at the back of Jake's head. Kacey had
come to him for protection. Not to her family. Not
to the feds. Not even to tribal police. To him, and
he was going to get to her with or without help. But
first he had to get out of this car.

KACEY WAS SURPRISED that she had no trouble finding
the house. Once there, they waited for FBI to swarm
the property. It looked like some scene from a movie
with grenade launchers throwing tear gas and men
and women in navy blue windbreakers approach-
ing the quiet house with guns drawn. The mailbox
lay broken on the curb and she realized it must have
been what she had crashed into. The eerie stillness
of the house disconcerted her. Shouldn't her friends
have been screaming when the gas poured into the
basement?

Her contractions had started up again, building
now and making her want to push. Word came back
that the house was empty.

"Empty? That's impossible."

"Are you sure this is the right house?" asked
Rivas.

Kacey glanced out the side window, recalling

running along that roof. "Yes, I'm sure. This is the house."

"All right. We're checking it out. Meanwhile, let's get you to the hospital to have this baby."

"The hospital. No. They'll find us there."

"You'll have protection twenty-four seven. FBI agents stationed outside your house."

"No. I want to go back to Colt."

Rivas gave her a sympathetic look. "Sweetie, he's mentally unstable. That's why he was discharged early. You know that, right?"

Kacey was shaking her head. "What happened to him?"

"He was captured by insurgents and held for three days with six of his unit. Record shows he was held under torture and was the only survivor. Afterward he couldn't adjust. He's seen mental health professionals there and here. He's received a psychiatric discharge and referral to seek help. But he has not done so. In fact, according to his brother, Colt has been home for four months but lives like a hermit and won't talk to his family. He's only been seen by the brother with the record…" Rivas rolled her eyes up as she tried to recall the name.

"Ty."

"Yes. Right. Ty Redhorse. Charged with armed robbery at eighteen. The tribe did not permit federal prosecution and charges were dropped in lieu of service in the US Marines. Known gang affiliations. No recent convictions or arrests." She smiled, as if pleased with her recall.

"If the tribe's gang is tied up in this, then you don't want to see or be seen by Ty," said Lieutenant Forrest from the front seat.

But Colt had called him, hadn't he?

"Do you know why you were impregnated?"

She shook her head. "Do you?"

"We have a theory based on the Caucasian infant born to Zella Colelay. Possible sale of fetal tissue."

"Tissue?" She clutched her stomach.

"That or human trafficking for surrogacy. We have a lot of questions for you. But we'll get you to the hospital first."

"In Darabee?" she asked, horrified.

"That's the closest medical facility."

"No. Not Darabee."

Rivas gave her a tight smile. "You need to relax, Kaccy. We got you."

Her words did not reassure Kacey. She sank back in the seat as she realized she had traded one prison for another.

"SHE'S IN DARABEE hospital," Jake told Colt.

"We have to get her out."

"Bear Den says she delivered in the ER. They just got her there in time."

"How do I get to her?"

"You don't. She's got FBI security."

"Kee works there," said Colt, referring to their oldest brother and the family's only MD. "He could get to her."

"Maybe, but he can't get her out of custody."

Colt pressed one fist into his opposite hand and brought them to his mouth, thinking.

"And why do you believe that she'll be safer with you than with the Bureau?" asked Jake.

"I don't. But she does."

"She might feel differently now…" Jake's words fell off.

"Now that she's seen me, you mean."

Jake shifted as if his clothing were suddenly uncomfortable. "Or she sees that the FBI can keep her safe."

"She's a captive again."

"Well, if there are people after her, she can't just go tramping around in the woods with you. She has a baby, Colt. Babies need somewhere warm and dry with a microwave to heat formula."

"Our ancestors raised us without all that."

"I know our history, brother," said Jake.

"I need to see Kacey."

"You need to see a psychiatrist."

Colt threw himself back against the rear seat, folding his arms before him. The ceiling of the car seemed lower than before and the buzzing in his ears escalated, making it harder and harder for him to think.

Finally, he said, "They have psychiatrists in Darabee."

Jake's eyes flashed to the rearview, meeting Colt's. "You'll see someone there?"

Colt nodded.

"This a trick to get to Kacey?"

"You said I have to see someone. So I'll see someone."

"Because of her."

"Everything I do from this second onward will be because of her." But the voice in his head whispered that he was not safe to be around a baby. What if he freaked out and hurt it during a panic attack?

"It's possible they will let you see her. But I wouldn't get my hopes up."

"Is Kee working there today?"

Jake shrugged. "Don't know his schedule." Jake passed Colt his mobile through the slot in the wire cage that separated the front from the rear seat of his police unit. "He's in my favorites." Jake gave Colt the pass code and Colt took the phone, staring at it for a moment. Then he cleared his throat several times. Finally, he lifted his chin, locked his teeth and made the call.

Kee only hesitated a moment before responding to Colt's request. Kee was at the tribe's health-care clinic today but said he'd see what he could find out. Jake accepted his phone back and used it to call his chief. He wanted assurances that if he brought Colt off their tribal lands, Colt would not be arrested. He listened and then disconnected.

"He's looking into it," Jake said.

Jake pulled over before leaving their lands, waiting for the call back. Colt asked to step out of the vehicle and hoped that Jake would refuse. He needed out but also knew if he was allowed to set foot on the ground, Jake would never get him back inside his police unit again.

Jake refused, thank God. The ceiling dropped another two inches and Colt had to hunch down below the seat to keep it from crushing him.

His brother pivoted in his seat and peered at him through the wire mesh. "What are you doing?" Colt was saved from answering by Jake's phone. "It's Kee."

Jake put the call on speaker.

"She's in Maternity," said Kee. "Mother and baby in good condition. Vaginal delivery. It's a boy."

"Hers?" asked Jake.

"Not sure," said Kee. "My colleague can't find anything out about the baby."

Jake scowled. "What colleague?"

"Dr. Hauser. He's in Darabee today."

Jake swore. Now Colt was scowling. Why did Jake have a problem with Hector Hauser? Hauser had been Kee's mentor and the one who had got him to the specialist who corrected Kee's leg-length discrepancy. He was also the head physician at the tribe's health-care clinic.

"Jake? Take me off speaker a minute."

Jake complied and held the phone to his ear.

"Yes. I know that." He paused to listen. "Seems so." Another pause. "Well, he's talking. I'd call that progress." Jake's gaze flicked to the rearview mirror and met Colt's eyes as he listened. "Maybe." Then another pause. "All right. See you there."

"See me where?" asked Colt.

"He wants us to stop by the urgent-care trailer."

"Trailer?"

"Everything is in Turquoise Ridge now. Temporary FEMA housing. You know about the dam, right?"

Colt nodded. Ty had told him.

"What's your problem with Hauser?" asked Colt.

Jake's gaze flicked away as he shook his head. "Can't say."

Police business, Colt knew. Active investigation was his best guess. What did this have to do with the clinic?

Colt sat back, thinking. He knew he had panic attacks. He knew they made him sweat and shake, but he always knew where he was. He never flashed back to that time. No breaks with reality. His reality was hard enough without jumping back to Afghanistan. Oh, he thought about it and dreamed about it. He knew he had issues and maybe he was a little paranoid. But one thing he was certain of was that visiting a woman in the maternity ward in Darabee did not require a stop in the tribe's urgent-care center in Turquoise Ridge.

Jake and Kee were about to throw a butterfly net over him. He knew that for sure. He had been getting better. The shakes were nearly gone. It was just driving in a damn car. He hated feeling trapped as he waited for something bad to happen.

And talking. His voice vibrating through his body

reminded him of the screaming of his fellows. Their cries vibrated the same damn way as if it were him screaming. Maybe it was.

He shouldn't have left her.

"Almost there," said Jake.

Chapter Five

Three hours later, Kacey was resting in the delivery room after bringing her baby into the world. They had placed the pink, wiggling infant on her chest and she examined the tiny fingers, counting each one. She cradled the wet head, misshapen by the process of birth.

He was very pink, had large dark blue eyes and damp fine black hair. In other words, he did not look like any of Kacey's brothers and sisters when they came home from the hospital.

"Does he look Apache to you?" she asked the nurse who had talked her through much of the delivery.

Kacey's body ached down there because she had come in too late for the pain medication. How long had she been in here? It couldn't have been more than an hour since they brought her in. They said she was fully dilated when she arrived, whatever that was.

The nurse peered down at the newborn and hesitated. "Well, I can't really say."

Couldn't say or wouldn't say.

"He's beautiful. I know that much." The nurse gave her a smile.

Kacey held her baby. So the speculation among the girls was true. None of them were carrying their own child. She glanced down at the infant, who stared steadily up at her.

So whose child was this that she had delivered? Hers, she decided. Every cell but two had come from the nourishment of her flesh. And this baby was hers.

The contractions began again. Then a nurse whisked him away to be cleaned up. Kacey reached after him.

"I want him in the room with me," she said.

The nurse cast Kacey a smile that seemed patronizing before she lifted the naked boy. "We'll bring him to you when he's hungry."

No. That was not good enough. She knew they wanted this baby. She still didn't know why. But they'd get him if she wasn't watching. "They'll take him."

Another nurse stepped before her. "Honey, we have tight security. No one gets near our babies except the mommy and daddy."

They would. She knew it. "It's not safe."

"Listen, nothing like what happened at your health clinic will happen here."

The fear moved from her stomach to her heart. "What happened at our health clinic?"

The doctor's brow furrowed. She was an older woman with a close-cut cap of dark curling hair and thin penciled brows. She had been very good at explaining things. "The two shooters who came in and tried to steal a baby. The one that police officer found in his truck."

Zella's baby? Her skin went cold. It proved her point. These people—the ones who had captured her, impregnated her and then held her against her will—were not going to let some little hospital keep them from getting that baby.

"Let me up," she said, taking her feet from the metal stirrups.

"You're delivering the afterbirth. You can't get up."

Kacey watched them care for her baby as the contractions gripped her again. The afterbirth came quickly and intact, according to the doctor. They massaged her stomach then. The doctor said that was to stop the bleeding.

Kacey endured the pain of this and then sat up.

"You should rest a bit. We'll be moving you to a room soon and you can clean up."

"With Charlie," she said.

"Is that what you're calling him?"

"Yes. I can name him, right?"

"Of course. If you plan on keeping him," said the doctor, her voice full of mirth. "Lie back down. They'll get you a bed and wheel you right to your room."

They wanted to take the baby to get shots and some other things while they took her to her room, but she refused to go. When they tried to cajole, she resisted, and when they ordered her to lie down, she pitched a fit that would have made any middle-school girl proud. She yelled so loud that an unfamiliar FBI agent, the female FBI agent Rivas and Jack Bear Den all came into the delivery room to check on them. And there she was, half-dressed, bloody and screaming like a wild woman.

The agent suggested they give her something, and that scared her into silence.

"We can't give her anything. Whatever you give her goes into her blood and right into her breast milk."

The agent made a face. Bear Den suggested they give her back her baby.

"We told her about the abduction attempt at your clinic," said one of the nurses.

"Brilliant," said Rivas.

Bear Den turned to Kacey. "We arrested and captured those two. They won't be coming for you or your baby."

"But someone will," she said.

"That's why we're here," Bear Den said.

Kacey demanded her baby and they finally turned him over.

In the end, they let her watch the processing of her child, including a heel prick for a blood sample that made him cry and the inking of his feet for a print. Shots, a sponge bath, a tiny bracelet on his ankle. She got a larger model. The nurse explained that the security bracelet kept anyone from taking the baby on the elevators, near the laundry chute or near the stairs.

"It locks them?" she asked.

"Elevators, yes."

So not the stairs.

"Can someone cut off the band?"

"The alarm sounds if it's not touching skin or if it's cut."

"Who has the key?"

"So many questions." The nurse's smile seemed fixed and her eyes tired.

The nurse showed her the key while another gave Charlie his first diaper and swaddling. At last, they put Charlie in her arms.

"He's not Apache. Is he?" she asked the doctor.

The woman peeled back the flannel blanket to peer at Charlie's face.

"I don't know. He sure could be."

She glanced to Jack Bear Den, who met her gaze and gave his head a slow shake, confirming Kacey's suspicions. She wasn't a mother. She was a surrogate.

"Will blood tests show if I'm his real mother?" she asked.

"They might," said the doctor.

"How long will that take?"

"Not long. We sent them up to the lab. Should hear back soon. Now you need to rest. We'll put Charlie in a bassinet right next to you in your room. How will that be?"

She nodded and allowed them to transfer her to a gurney. She held Charlie as they transported her to a single room with the agents that walked with her and stopped outside her private room. A glance at the window showed the tops of trees and the strip mall across the parking lot and street. She was on the third or fourth floor.

The attendant showed her how to use the button to call the nurse. He offered to put Charlie in the bassinet beside her bed, but she rejected the suggestion. She was keeping him with her until they let her out—if they let her out.

Colt refused to go to the urgent-care center in Turquoise Ridge. It was the wrong direction, for a start. Kacey was in Darabee. But Jake would not let him out of his police unit. By the time he got to the Turquoise Ridge urgent-care center, he was throwing himself against the cage between the front and rear seat like a feral animal. He told himself to stop, but the screaming in his head had taken him. He was on his back on the back seat, preparing to kick out the rear window, when Jake pulled over.

"Okay. You can get out."

Colt righted himself. They were in a wide field filled with trailers. They sprang up in the yellow grass of the open field like white mushrooms on a rotting log. Jake opened the rear door and Colt dived through the opening and ran. Jake shouted after him, but he ran and kept running until he was far enough away from the gas tank and the vehicle to be safe from explosions.

There he stopped, hands on knees. He panted. Sweated. His sides ached. But he could breathe again. Dry air, but cool. Not like Afghanistan.

"Colt," called Jake from his position halfway between his police cruiser and his younger brother. He motioned with one arm. "Come back."

Kee jogged out and stopped beside Jake, watching him. Behind him, coming at a walk, was a woman Colt did not know. Colt retraced his steps, giving the cruiser a wide berth. His throat was so dry.

They wanted him to go inside one of the trailers. He walked the perimeter first. No engine. But there was a generator outside that ran on gas.

"You'll have to see me here." Colt sat in the grass.

All three of them stared at him. They then shared a silent exchange that involved long glances and head gestures.

In the end, they did as he asked and gave him what the marine doctors had given him. A prescription for antidepressants, sleeping pills and an appointment to see a shrink. He sagged with relief. Now he had to get to Kacey.

Colt thanked them. But then he had to face Jake's car again. He started sweating. He hated himself as he considered asking for the shot. The one they'd used to transport him back home and to get him safely to Phoenix. He'd walked from there to Turquoise Canyon. It had taken eight days.

But if he took that medicine, he'd be good for no one, especially not Kacey. Still, walking to her would take hours. So he asked them for a phone and he called his brother Ty.

Ty listened and agreed to help, as he always did. Colt wanted to go to Kacey, but Kenshaw was right. First he needed to help himself. The FBI was guarding her. They were better able to keep her safe. He knew that. It was reasonable. Rational. So why did he feel so uneasy? Because, just like last time, she had come to him for help and he had let her down, again.

He heard the familiar roar of a Harley long before he saw his brother Ty. Colt's older brother ignored the curb and rolled right up beside him where he sat on the grass surrounded by medical professionals, tribal police and his brothers Jake and Kee.

Ty ignored them all and spoke only to Colt. "You driving or should I?"

Colt stood.

"I think we should admit him," said Kee to Ty.

"Yeah? What does he think?" asked Ty, looking at Colt.

Colt shook his head.

"We only need two family members to sign the papers," said Jake, siding with Kee as usual.

"Screw that," said Ty, straddling the bike with one booted foot planted firmly on each side. He dismounted, holding the bike with one hand as he looked to Colt.

"You drive," he said.

"At least let Kenshaw speak to him," said Kee.

"You know where to find him," said Ty.

Colt straddled the bike and turned the key. The motor roared to life.

"Go on," said Ty.

Chapter Six

Colt drove to Darabee on the 1990 Harley-Davidson Heritage Softail in the early afternoon. The bike was cream and coffee with a maroon pinstripe and enough chrome to resurface the top of the Chrysler Building. This was Ty's pride and joy and had been refurbished with love. More important, Colt felt none of the anxiety and claustrophobia when riding in the open air on the chopper.

Why hadn't he tried this sooner?

Because he had no reason to leave the ridge. That was the answer. Kacey had given him a reason to leave, to fight and to come back to the world.

He sailed into Darabee and parked in the hospital lot but got as far as the lobby, where FBI agents waited and were disinclined to let him pass. He used the hospital phone to call her room but got no answer. He didn't leave a message. He was still waiting in the lobby when the world outside the lobby windows faded with the daylight. The first of the outside lights had just flickered on when Kenshaw Little Falcon arrived with Colt's brother Jake. Kenshaw was the tribe's shaman, a licensed therapist and a longtime friend of the family.

"They won't let me see her," he said.

Jake's mouth was a slashing grim line. "Because they think you're a threat."

"Threat's out there," said Colt.

"Are you armed?" asked Jake.

Colt shook his head. "You got my pistol, and my rifle was in my truck."

"Knives?"

"No." It was a fair question because both he and Jake knew that Colt threw a knife with the accuracy that some shot arrows.

"They'll come for her," Colt told Jake.

"Don't you worry about that," said Jake. "The FBI is guarding her."

"She's Turquoise Canyon. *We* should be guarding her."

Colt had done more talking today than the sum total since he'd been released from the hospital in Bethesda, Maryland.

"How long will she be here?" he asked.

Jake rubbed his neck, tipping his Stetson down

over his eyes. "Don't know. I do know that she's in the delivery room."

"You think they'll try to keep her?"

"Not your worry. Besides, that's up to her. She agreed to protection."

What other choice had she had? Him? He must have seemed a lunatic in her eyes. Colt stared at the polished tile floor and swallowed at the lump in his throat. "She came to me for help."

"After she tried the old tribal headquarters. No one was there. This is not your fight, Colt."

Kenshaw motioned to the chair beside the end table, perpendicular to the one Colt had vacated. "Mind if I wait with you?"

Colt had always liked and respected their shaman. He radiated calm and strength.

"I'd like that," said Colt and resumed his seat.

Jake's brows lifted.

"Why don't you see if you can get an update on Kacey? See how she's doing and if she needs anything from us," said their shaman to Jake.

Dismissed, Jake spun away and headed for the elevators. The two agents posted by them delayed Jake briefly before allowing him to pass.

Kenshaw rested his hands on the armrests of the chair and said nothing. The shaman had a way of blending with his surroundings instead of taking them over until it was almost as if he was not even there.

Colt looked out the window to the darkness broken by streetlights in the parking lot while he tried to imagine he sat in his place in the woods.

Colt's father had made the mining cabin with his brother using planed pine obtained from the tribe's lumber mill. Colt never asked how they got the lumber but recalled helping them load it well past dark. Building the mining cabins was as close to honest work, as far as Colt was aware, as his father had ever done. His father now resided in federal prison in Phoenix on a final robbery charge that tipped the scales from misdemeanor to felony and serious jail time. It had taken his mom three years after that to decide to divorce him.

Colt wished he could divorce himself from the name they'd given him. Colton Redhorse, Jr., a chip off the old block. He'd spent a lot of his teen years tipping between proving folks right or wrong. If not for Ty riding him and Kee encouraging him, he never would have finished high school.

Colt glanced at his silent companion.

Kenshaw Little Falcon had not aged a day since Colt had last seen him. He still had long hair streaked with gray and a face that showed hard lines around his mouth and forehead. Gravity tugged at his jowls and made rings around his neck. His body was trim and strong, and he dressed like a rancher rather than the holy man that he was.

Colt found he did not mind the older man's presence in his space. But Colt's mind was with Kacey and his plans to get to her. He suspected she was in a lock-in floor. What was the best way to get her out?

"Sometimes the only way out is through," said Kenshaw, replying to the question that Colt had not voiced.

Colt's brow wrinkled as he stared at the holy man. Had that been a lucky guess?

"To see her, you will have to prove you are not a danger to her or yourself. And it will have to be her wish. Not just yours."

His shaman decided to speak in Tonto Apache then. It had been Kenshaw who had taught them all the language of their birth, and he spoke to Colt now, telling him of the dam disaster and how Colt's brother Jake had saved the FBI explosives agent, Sophia Rivas, from the police boat after the explosion she and Detective Bear Den had initiated to save them from the flood.

He talked a long time, and Colt did not feel anxious or have to resist the urge to walk off in the woods to get away from him. Instead, he had to resist the urge to start walking toward Piñon Forks and the tribe's fight to reinforce the rubble dam.

Finally, they got back to Colt's troubles. Colt told him some of it, nothing that everyone didn't already know.

When he finished, Kenshaw nodded. "I can see why you stay up there. You have a lot to work through. I'd like to help. I am a therapist, but I know a good man, a veteran who also suffered some losses."

"All right." Colt needed to quiet the screaming in his head. He needed to get to Kacey and be there when she needed him.

Colt told Kenshaw what Kacey had told him about her capture and imprisonment.

"She's not on our land," said Colt. "She's out here and she's a captive again. I believe what she said. They won't let her go or let her keep her baby."

"She want to keep it?" Kenshaw asked.

"She should have that choice."

"And why are you better suited to protect her than our tribal police?"

"They follow the law, while I will do whatever it takes to defend her."

"You would break the law," he said.

Colt inclined his head. No question. No hesitation.

Kenshaw gave him a long contemplative gaze. Finally, he nodded and sat back in his chair. Then he laced his gnarled thick fingers over his flat stomach. "To care for others, you first must be capable of caring for yourself."

"I know that. It's why I agreed to see your therapist."

"Then I'll help you," said their shaman.

Kenshaw made no move to depart. Eventually the elevator doors opened and Jake emerged from within. Colt was on his feet as Jake approached.

"How is she?" Colt asked.

"She's still in the delivery room."

"Who's watching her?"

"Detective Bear Den."

Her pursuers would be checking maternity wards. Colt resumed his seat.

"You going to sit there all night?" asked Jake.

Colt planned to do just that.

Three hours later, Detective Bear Den strode from the elevators, holding his hat like a football against his side. Kenshaw had gone a little after midnight and Colt was alone except for the FBI agents at the elevator, the receptionist and security guard.

Colt rose to his feet, staring at the detective as he tried to ascertain at a glance if Kacey was all right. "How is she?"

"She had the baby."

"She okay?"

"Fine. Normal delivery. The baby is healthy."

Colt squinted. He'd said that twice now—*the baby*. Not *her baby* or *Kacey's baby*. "Hers?"

Bear Den didn't answer. Colt put a hand on his arm, and the detective looked at it and then at Colt.

Bear Den's scowl deepened. "Blood work shows it's not Kacey's."

"She delivered it."

"She's a surrogate, just like Zella Colelay."

That was the girl who had left the newborn in his brother's truck. Kacey said Zella knew her from school, but Colt didn't remember her.

"FBI is expediting DNA testing."

"Can I see her?" asked Colt.

"She's sleeping."

"Not what I asked."

Bear Den scraped his knuckles over the stubble on his jaw. "Not my call. Forrest says you stay off the maternity ward."

"What do you say?"

"Let her rest."

Colt remained standing. "Anything on her friends?"

"We got zip." Bear Den shifted and glanced to the door. "You should go home and get some rest."

"I'm staying."

"See you in the morning." Bear Den replaced his

hat on his head, pressed it down with one giant hand and strode through the exit.

Colt resumed his seat.

Colt saw the shift change at six in the morning when two new FBI field agents replaced the old. He was sitting on a stool at the hospital cafeteria lunch counter nursing some weak coffee when Detective Bear Den and his brother Jake arrived. Jake was in his tribal police uniform, his name tag on the left breast pocket, handgun on his hip and his hair drawn neatly back in a single braid. Unlike Ty, Jake radiated his emotions, so Colt knew there was trouble before Bear Den spoke. The muscles between Colt's shoulders hitched as he braced in preparation.

He took the seat one away from Colt.

"You still talking this morning?" Jake asked.

Colt said nothing. Jake swiped his hand over his mouth and ordered black coffee from the server behind the counter. She brought it promptly and set it before him with a napkin.

He took a swallow of the coffee and winced. "I told Ma you're down off the ridge. She wants to come see you, but you know Burt has the truck and she can't drive because, you know, her medical issues."

Colt said nothing, but he knew his mother's vision was not good because of the diabetes and that she'd had two toes amputated because of the same illness.

"Any chance you could stop up to the house?"

Colt spun his stool back to face the counter and his cold cup of coffee. "You going up to see her?"

Jake stood. "Yeah. Kenshaw signed off that you're no threat to Kacey. I'm the delivery boy." Jake patted the papers protruding from his rear pocket.

Colt had not even known that he was being evaluated.

He followed Jake as far as the elevator, where he waited for the doors to open and close and take his brother to Kacey. If they didn't let him up there soon, he was going to blow Kenshaw's faith in him by doing something stupid.

AFTER THE NIGHT in the hospital, Kacey woke up with a new heaviness in her breasts and some soreness down there. She was surprised to see daylight outside her window. How long had she been asleep?

Where was Charlie?

They'd taken her baby twice so far for changing, but they'd always brought Charlie right back.

She tried to sit up, but the soreness made her gasp. On her second try, she rolled to her side and swung her legs gingerly off the bed. The agents posted at her door looked surprised at her appearance but only shadowed her as she shuffled down the hall. She tracked Charlie down to the nursery and found a nurse feeding him from a bottle. Her eyes narrowed.

Kacey crashed her open hand against the glass viewing window and shouted, making both nurses inside the room jump.

The one who was not holding Charlie came to speak to her. "We didn't want to wake you."

"If he's hungry, you bring him to me," she said.

The nurse looked confused. "But you told us you don't want to breastfeed."

A tingle of alarm trickled down her spine. "When did I say that?"

Chapter Seven

The nurse gave Kacey a look of bafflement at her question. She had not told anyone that she did not want to breastfeed her baby.

"It's in your chart."

"It's a lie. Give him to me."

Kacey tried to push past the nurse to get to Charlie, but the nurse blocked her way to the door.

"You can't go in there."

Kacey rounded on the nurse, preparing to fight. The nurse must have seen the crazy in Kacey's eyes because she lifted her hands in instant surrender.

"Clean environment," she said, hurrying her words. "You have to wear a mask and…let me just… I'll bring him out."

Kacey lowered her chin and glared. "Do it."

The tightness in her chest eased as they slipped Charlie back into her arms. He fussed at having his meal interrupted and Kacey felt the flow of milk in her breasts.

She turned to the agents. "I want to see Colt Red-horse."

"No visitors, ma'am."

"You get me your supervisor or I walk out of here right now."

The men exchanged a look. Perhaps the idea of tackling a mother holding an infant gave them pause. They eyed her warily but did not reply to her demand.

"Fine," she said and marched past them. She only got two steps before one of the matched pair stepped before her and the other spoke.

"I'll call our supervisor."

"Now," she said.

Kacey took Charlie back to her room and fed him. Was it just a mistake or did someone want to replace her with a bottle? Was it the FBI or the Russians? She examined the security bracelet on Charlie's ankle. There was no way to get it off without cutting it and then the alarm would alert them all.

Charlie yawned and Kacey adjusted the cotton cap on his head. A few minutes later, FBI field agent Lieutenant Luke Forrest appeared. He said he was against letting her see Colt. He offered a visit from her mother or sisters. Tempting, but endangering her sisters was not on the list. And seeing her mother would bring more drama than she could handle right now. Did the FBI know about her drug use? She didn't think so. There would be nothing to see in a background search, as her mom had never been arrested, though it had been close.

What Kacey needed was someone she trusted. That was a short list. Marta Garcia, still with her captors, and Colt Redhorse.

"Colt," she said.

He gave her a long assessing stare. "We can protect you, Kacey."

"You're Apache," she said. "You understand my reluctance to surrender to federal authorities. And as a member of the Turquoise Canyon Apache people, I have certain rights." She played the only card she had and then stopped talking.

"You sure he's the guy? He's been less than stable."

"He's the guy."

BEFORE THEY BROUGHT her lunch tray, there was a commotion outside her room.

"One at a time," said the new guard who stood in the hall before her door.

"We're tribal police," said a familiar voice. That was Colt's brother Jake.

"One."

A moment later, in stepped Colt Redhorse. Suddenly she wasn't afraid anymore. Colt was here. She reached for him, her stomach aching in protest. He clasped her hand and then lifted it to his mouth, dropping a warm kiss there. Her skin tingled at the contact. She squeezed his fingers and tugged, drawing him closer, and he sat on the bed beside her hip.

"You all right?" he asked.

She shook her head. "They want to take him."

His dark brows descended. "Who?"

Again she shook her head. "Something is happening," she said. Then she told him about the bottle-feeding.

He did not dismiss her concerns. Instead he said, "We need to get you home."

Home was exactly where they would look for her. She shook her head. "They'll find me there."

Colt drew his hand away and rubbed it on his thigh. "Jake said you were considering relocation with the Justice Department."

Cold panic surged. "They said that? I haven't made up my mind yet. All I said was that I would help them find my friends. But I need to protect Charlie, too."

He blinked at this. "Charlie. Is that his name?"

She nodded, waiting for his reaction. He looked

away, staring off at nothing she could determine. Then his gaze swept back to hers. "I like it."

"Would you like to hold him?"

Colt straightened, his warm smile replaced by an expression of alarm.

"Put out your arms," she said.

He did, looking as if she were going to load them with firewood. She shifted forward so that her shoulder grazed his as she set her baby in his arms. His gaze dropped to the boy's tiny face. Charlie gazed up in wonder at this new person.

"Hi," breathed Colt.

There was a tug in her chest as she watched them together. Colt stared a long time and Charlie stared right back. Colt used one finger to connect with Charlie's tiny hand. Her son grasped the offered finger and Colt laughed.

"He's strong!" He flicked his gaze to hers, giving her that lopsided smile she had loved. "He's perfect, Kacey."

She stroked her baby's soft cheek with one finger. "They told me that he's not mine by blood."

His smile faltered.

"But he's mine by birth and I am not giving him to the Russians."

He nodded and brought Charlie closer to him. "I'll help you protect him, Kacey."

"We have to get Charlie out of here."

"They can't keep you if you want to go home."

"I think they can. I heard one of the agents say I'm a material witness to a surrogacy ring."

Colt glanced toward the door. "I'll get you out."

Suddenly the world seemed a little brighter, like he had poked pinholes in the blackness that shrouded her and sunlight poured in. "You will?"

"Yes. You and Charlie."

"How?"

LATE MONDAY AFTERNOON, Colt had not left Kacey's room except to speak to Kenshaw right outside her door. Their shaman had agreed with Colt's suggestion on freeing Kacey from custody. The matter was complicated by her currently being off their tribal lands, but Kenshaw believed they might still gain her transfer to Turquoise Canyon.

Charlie stayed in the room with them, and when the nurses took him, Colt went with them. When they objected, Kacey insisted and he was permitted to shadow Charlie.

By midday, Jake appeared in the doorway. He motioned to Colt with his head. In the hall, Colt discovered Detective Bear Den waiting. The three men walked far enough from the guarding agents to avoid being overheard but within sight of Kacey's room. To ensure their privacy, they spoke in Apache.

"Can we get her out?" asked Colt.

"Working on it," said Jake.

"There's a problem," said Bear Den.

Colt's body braced and he glanced toward Kacey's room.

"We just got a call from Eddie SaVala," said Bear Den.

Eddie was the brother of his neighbor, David.

"He said he found his brother dead in his cabin. Someone shot him twice in the head."

A cold chill slithered down Colt's spine.

"FBI know yet?" asked Colt.

Bear Den shook his head.

"They're looking for Kacey," said Colt.

"Who is?" asked Jake.

"Her captors."

"That makes sense," said Bear Den. "From what we can see, they beat David first."

To get information, Colt thought. His mind provided a perfect memory of the sounds of his comrades screaming under torture. He pushed it aside. No time for the past right now. "Were they at my place?"

"No."

He closed his eyes and thanked David SaVala for his sacrifice.

"Any idea why they'd think Kacey was at SaVala's?"

"We borrowed his phone to call Jake."

"Why didn't you use your phone?" asked Jake.

"I don't have one," said Colt.

Bear Den scowled. "It's not easy to track the location of a mobile phone or figure out who owns it."

The implication was clear. Someone who could do that was very dangerous.

Colt suppressed the urge to run back to Kacey. "She's been here too long."

"She might be better off with the FBI," said Bear Den.

"She might be or with Justice," said Jake. "They can put her in witness protection, safeguard her identity."

"Make her disappear," added Bear Den.

Colt recalled that Bear Den's twin, Carter, and Carter's wife, Amber, had been in that program. Ty had told him about it. Everyone thought that they'd never see them again.

He didn't want Kacey to disappear. She'd only just returned and her arrival gave him a reason to try again. If she left, he'd just go back to that cabin and mining turquoise. There was satisfaction in striking those rocks. But nothing compared to holding Charlie or seeing Kacey's smile again.

"She's Turquoise Canyon Apache," said Colt, as if that were a reason to stay where there was danger. His heart was tripping along as if engaged in a long run. Had Kacey found her way off the rez? She'd always wanted to leave their mountains and had begged him to take her away, but he wanted to stay on their lands.

Turquoise Canyon was his home, and coming back to it was all that had kept him from losing his mind during those three terrible days.

Now he found himself in the same place again, convincing Kacey to come home when that might not be what was best for her and her son.

"We have to make a decision," said Jake. "Taking her out of federal custody might be a bad move."

"If her captors don't know she's here, they will soon," said Bear Den.

"They'd have to be crazy to come here. They've got four agents guarding her," said Jake. "She should stay here."

"Back home, the gang can get to her," said Bear Den. "We know that two known members, Earle Glass and Minnie Cobb, are involved."

Colt knew from Kenshaw that these two had tried

to snatch Jake's new baby, the one Zella had given birth to, and were now in federal custody.

"They won't know she's there."

Jake scoffed. "You borrowing your brother's bike was a bad move. Might as well have sent the gang a telegram."

Colt's jaw tightened. Everyone knew Ty had been a member of the tribe's gang. He wasn't now.

"He doesn't roll with them anymore," said Colt.

"Not according to the feds," said Bear Den.

Jake had told him that Bear Den was now formally engaged to the FBI explosives expert, Sophia Rivas. Had she told him something? Colt pressed down the doubt. He didn't know if Ty was tangled up with the Wolf Posse again. He did know that Ty had his back. Hadn't he turned over his bike to help Colt get to Darabee?

But had he then gone to Pike and reported Colt and Kacey's location? Faras Pike was the tribal gang's leader and once the best friend of his brother Ty, back when they were both new recruits of the Wolf Posse. Once Ty had said they were his family. Were they still?

"This means they were on our land," said Bear Den. "I've got to notify the FBI about the death of David SaVala. They might want to move Kacey to a safe house."

"Kee told me she should have been released by now," said Jake. "You know any reason they haven't moved her already?"

"We have to get her out of here," said Colt.

"That's impossible," said Bear Den.

"She thinks the FBI will take her into custody and separate her from her child."

Jake gaped at him. His eyes flicked to Bear Den's and held.

Bear Den dismissed the idea. "That's crazy."

Colt told them about the chart and how they seemed to be weaning Charlie away from Kacey. The men scowled.

"You have any reason to doubt her?" Colt asked.

"Test results indicate the child's genetic lineage is Asian and Caucasian," said Bear Den.

Colt's gaze flashed to Jake, who looked just as off balance at this announcement.

"In other words, it's not her child," said Bear Den.

Colt dug in his heels. "She carried it. She delivered it. If she says the baby is hers, that's all I need to know."

Bear Den made a face. "You're borrowing trouble."

"Bring it."

"Fine. *If* she wants out. But you'll need help."

"My brothers," said Colt.

"The tribe," said Bear Den. "You need the backing of the tribal council. That's the only way I know to get her past security or away from the FBI."

"This means we lose FBI protection," said Jake. He turned to Colt. "You sure about this?"

He wasn't. She had told him often before he joined the Marines that she wanted to be away from their tribe and her mother and everyone who thought she was nothing and no one. Did that list now include him?

Chapter Eight

Colt had given Kacey the options of staying with the FBI or coming home to Turquoise Canyon. He said that Kenshaw would invoke the protection of Tribal Thunder. She knew that name. It was the warrior sect of the tribe's medicine society. The men and women of this group had taken a vow to protect their people. Was her tribe's warrior sect strong enough to protect her from what Luke Forrest had identified as the Russian mob? Agent Forrest had assured her that his agency had not changed those orders regarding the birth mother's wishes about the infant's feeding. But someone had.

He was arranging discharge from the hospital and removal to a safe house. Unlike Colt, Forrest did not offer her a choice, which made her decision easier.

By noon on Tuesday, Kacey was dressed and ready as she waited for the delegation from her tribe to arrive to demand custody of both mother and child.

Unfortunately, either the FBI got wind of their plans or their timing just stank, because she was informed by the hospital staff that she was being moved. Colt had contacted the tribal council, but when the FBI came for her, it was just her and Colt. It took three agents to hold Colt down.

Kacey held her baby and screamed for them to release Colt, but it did no good. One of the nurses appeared and Kacey braced to fight her off until she saw the key and realized the nurse was here to unlock the security bracelets on mother and child. Once free, Kacey's instinct was to protect the baby and that kept her from going to Colt's aid. In her moment of indecision, two agents took hold of her arms. They were taking her.

She held Charlie and called to Colt as she was marched out past Jake Redhorse, who was arguing and talking on his radio simultaneously.

"Jake, stop them. Don't let them take me."

They hustled her down the corridor and to the elevators. Her heart hammered in her chest. What was happening? The agents accompanying her would not answer her questions, and their grips on her arms made it clear they thought she'd run.

They rushed her down a long corridor and out a side door. There she found a single black sedan waiting with an agent standing beside the open rear door.

She knew if she got in that car she wouldn't see Colt or her people again and she feared that they might take Charlie from her. She dug in her heels. This slowed them not at all.

Three familiar tribal police units arrived. From one SUV came Detective Bear Den and tribal police chief Wallace Tinnin, who leaned on a single crutch. Two uniformed tribal officers emerged from the police unit behind that one. From the next came a third tribal police officer who opened the door for the tribe's executive director, Zach Gill. The FBI was now outnumbered.

A side door banged open and out rushed Colt, a handcuff dangling from one wrist. He didn't slow as he covered the ten yards that separated them with astonishing speed.

One of the agents turned when Colt made his tackle. The man holding her opposite arm released her to help his companion, drawing his pistol.

Kacey took a step toward Colt, remembered she held Charlie and froze. Bear Den called a warning to the agent to holster his weapon, his hand on his own.

"He's unarmed," called Tinnin.

Colt now had the agent on his back and was straddling his waist, holding both arms pinned. He'd been a wrestler in high school, she recalled, a very good one.

Tinnin and Jake Redhorse were at Kacey's side.

They hustled her and Charlie into the tribal SUV. Bear Den waited until she was in the back seat before calling Colt off.

Colt released the agent, who scrambled to his feet as Colt charged toward Kacey. Tinnin used his crutch as a barricade between the agent and Colt, who hurried into the SUV with her.

"He's under arrest," said the agent.

"Come and get him," said Bear Den.

The agent pointed at Kacey. "She's a material witness. We have custody."

Tinnin shook his head. "You might think twice before you touch anyone in that vehicle. That car constitutes sovereign land, an extension of our reservation."

Colt's breathing wasn't slowing down.

"You saved us," she whispered.

Colt was sweating and hugging himself now. The closed vehicle, she realized, was affecting him again. She wrapped her free arm around him and he rested his head on her.

Bear Den slipped behind the wheel and set them in motion.

She spun to look back at the three agents facing off against Gill, Tinnin and Colt's brother Jake.

Had she made a mistake, choosing her tribe? After

all, they'd done little to protect her during her childhood and she had needed protecting often.

"Is that true about the sovereignty of this vehicle?"

"Not that I'm aware," Bear Den said.

The agents had a choice between drawing their weapons or their phones. One lifted his phone as they made the turn from the hospital to the street.

"They'll come after us," said Kacey.

"Then we best get to Turquoise Canyon," said Bear Den.

She sat in the back holding her baby boy. No one was taking Charlie from her again. Not the nurses or doctors or the Russians who had held her captive.

Colt's eyes rounded and the rocking turned to a steady banging of his shoulder against the side door as if he was trying to batter it open while holding himself back.

"Colt," she said.

He turned, the whites around his dark irises making him look like a frightened horse.

"Hold Charlie for me?"

He looked at the newborn and shook his head.

She laid her baby in his lap. He hesitated only a moment and then cradled him close but not tight.

Charlie was awake and fussing. Colt stroked his cheek, and her baby opened his eyes, staring up at

Colt in wonder. Colt smiled. His rocking now was forward and back and completely appropriate. Kacey breathed away a sigh of relief.

A smile curled Colt's lips. If not for the sweat beading on his forehead, he would look the picture of peace. Even his breathing was changing, slowing back to normal.

She glanced up to see the detective's reflection in the rearview mirror. He nodded at her and then returned his attention to the road.

This time, when they traveled through Piñon Forks, she took note of the huge section of rock missing from the canyon wall across the river. How had she missed that? She tried to imagine seeing that collapse under explosives set by the FBI agent. The rubble dam was visible from the road, leaking water, but holding back a lake from the river town. Men worked with heavy equipment, scrambling like ants to shore up the temporary structure.

En route to Koun'nde, Bear Den told her about the murder of Colt's neighbor, David SaVala. She remembered borrowing his phone.

"We killed him," she whispered.

"No. The people who are after you did that," Bear Den said. "It's not safe at Colt's cabin."

It wasn't safe anywhere. Not as long as they were hunting her.

"Where will we go?" She couldn't go to her mother's house. That would put all her brothers and sisters in danger. And truly, she didn't completely trust her mother.

"We meet at the tribal gathering place. They've invoked the protection of Tribal Thunder."

If anyone needed protection now, it was she and Charlie.

THEY REACHED THE river and Kacey breathed a sigh of relief. She was home again, but the feeling of security was an illusion. The Russians were hunting her.

Still, she was glad to arrive at the familiar gathering grounds. This was where she had danced all night for her Sunrise Ceremony, the Apache girls' coming-of-age celebration. She still had her white buckskin dress and the fan of eagle feathers she had carried as she transformed to Changing Woman to bring blessings to her people.

She had made the dress herself, as her mother had been gone again. Her favorite teacher had helped her and had come with the gifts that Changing Woman was expected to distribute to her tribe during the ceremony. Mrs. Trans had kept her from embarrassment, and her mother, who did make the ceremony, had pretended all the while, as Kacey carried the basket full of treats, that she was responsible for the bounty. Her mother's actions might have embarrassed Kacey more than having nothing to offer.

Bear Den pulled in and Colt slipped Charlie back into her arms.

"Thank you," he said. "I didn't think I could make that ride again."

Bear Den opened Colt's door first, as if anxious to be rid of him. Colt stepped out, glanced back at her and then made for the woods.

"Wait!" Kacey called.

He didn't and he didn't look back. Members of her tribe stepped forward, surrounding the SUV and blocking her view of him. The detective opened her door and she stepped onto tribal lands once more.

She was first formally greeted by their shaman, Kenshaw Little Falcon. Her mother was there and her young brothers, Jeffrey, who was eight, and Hewitt, who had turned five without her there. Her sisters, Jackie, Winnie and Shirley, each hugged her in turn. It struck her then, looking at them, that they had all changed. Jackie, now sixteen, had cut her hair short as if in mourning, and Shirley, now eleven, was very thin. Winnie, just past thirteen, had grown several inches. Kacey realized suddenly that she had missed Winnie's Sunrise Ceremony. Had Mrs. Trans been there to help her?

Her throat constricted at the loss of those precious months of her captivity and at the joy of seeing them again. Her next thought was for her friends, still in captivity.

As she hugged her mother, her resolve hardened to flint. She must help the FBI find her friends and bring them home.

Her sisters fussed over Charlie. Hewitt nudged between them, standing on his toes to look. Kacey's proud smile dropped when she saw her mother staring at Charlie. Her expression made it seem as if she smelled something bad and she refused when Kacey asked if she wished to hold Charlie.

"Held enough babies in my time," she said.

That rejection hurt as much as any her mother had ever given her. But she bit down, clenching her jaw as she held Charlie out for them to see. She hadn't needed her mother's approval to get her first job or apply for college. She certainly didn't need it now.

"Is that my baby brother?" Hewitt asked, peering at the baby.

"Well, no." Kacey glanced to her mother, who looked away.

"That is your nephew," said her sister Shirley, with no hint of shame or hesitation. "You are an uncle, Hewitt."

"I am?" He glanced back at their mother.

"If she says so," said her mother.

Hewitt beamed, then leaned down to kiss the baby.

And just like that, she and Charlie were accepted by her brother. Kacey offered her mother a smile of thanks and she nodded in return. Her mother had not always been there for them and she had her problems. Kacey hoped that accepting her baby into the family would not be one of them.

The October sun filtered down through the trees and glowed golden on the tribe's open gathering ground. She was escorted by her two youngest sisters, Shirley and Winnie, to the center of the dance circle. There she was formally welcomed home by Hazel Trans, now a new member of the tribal council, who spoke in place of Zach Grill, their executive director, who had aided in Kacey's escape. It occurred to Kacey that Mrs. Trans had been in her last year of teaching and was now retired. A loss, thought Kacey. It was Hazel Trans who had encouraged her to take the SATs after Colt left for the US Marines. It was because of Mrs. Trans that Kacey had been accepted into the university. Her head dropped an inch in regret as she realized she had missed the start of her freshman year.

Kacey held Charlie as she pictured what had been stolen from her. It had been all she wanted in the world, to go off the rez and earn her degree and be able to support herself. She wanted to create the stable home her mother never provided and then help her sisters make their own way. Now her aspirations were changing. Now all she wanted was to keep Charlie safe and out of the hands of the men who hunted her.

She glanced around for Colt. He had left the car with her, but now he had vanished. Was he watching from somewhere away from the crowd?

Hazel Trans finished her welcome and stepped aside to allow Kenshaw Little Falcon to speak. He told the gathering that this baby had not been Kacey's choice but that he was here now in this world with them and he was Turquoise Canyon Apache by birth. Because he was one of them, they would protect him. It was a sacred duty shared by all, to keep their young safe and teach them well. Kacey looked down at the subject of their speeches. Charlie yawned and squinted against the sunlight.

After Kenshaw completed his short speech, he offered a formal blessing using a fan of eagle feathers. His voice turned to a song rising to the blue sky.

When he finished, Kenshaw told them all that the men who had taken Kacey were outsiders with Russian accents. If they saw such men on their land, they were to call the police.

By the time all the well-wishers had spoken to Kacey and offered their advice on the baby, she was past exhausted. When Charlie fussed, Kacey's mother offered her a blanket to provide her some privacy as she nursed.

She released her baby only to allow her sisters Jackie and Winnie to change him with her overseeing the proceedings. They both had changed Hewitt and Jeffrey in the past. Jackie, the next oldest to Kacey, was the same age and class as Brenda Espinoza, still in captivity. Kacey prayed their captors had not harmed any of them because of her.

When Zach Gill arrived at last, he and Kenshaw got all but the most stubborn visitors back into their trucks and off the gathering grounds just in time to keep them from setting up a drum circle and camping there for the night. Kacey said goodbye to her family and was shown to a cabin. She paused to glance back at the lodge where the council conducted business.

There on the wide porch gathered some of her tribe members who had remained behind. A few of the faces were familiar. She recognized three of them because they were members of their nationally known hotshot team. This was her tribe's elite wildfire squad distinguished nationwide. She had met Carter Bear Den, Ray Strong and Dylan Tehauno. She also knew the woman beside Jake, Lori Redhorse, who was a nurse at the tribe's health-care clinic, where Kacey suspected this had all begun. Kacey remembered then that Jake had told Colt that he had made Lori his wife.

The chief of tribal police, Wallace Tinnin, nodded at her from his place between Carter and Jack Bear Den. Amber Bear Den, Carter's wife, held her husband's arm, and Ray's wife, Morgan Strong, stood to her right with her eyes on the river. There were others Kacey did not know, but they all looked toward her. And then she realized exactly who they were.

Tribal Thunder.

This was the warrior sect of the Turquoise Guardians, the protectors, drawn into service to keep her safe. She had been told they would watch over her, but she had never seen them before today. These were the best of their numbers, hand-selected for their bravery and dedication to their tribe. She scanned the faces for Colt and did not find him or his brother Ty or Kee. Only Jake Redhorse stood among the warrior sect of her people.

Kacey raised her free hand in salute and then carried her son into the cabin where they would stay until their safety could be assured. She wanted to trust them, but her experience was that the tribe had not been there to help her or her siblings when her mother had left them for days and days. Protective services had come and gone, taking them from and returning them to their mother as if they were sheep changing pastures. It had got worse until finally her only option was to leave this place.

She'd hoped to convince Colt to come with her. But he'd had his own plans for them that included her staying put for two more years. Kacey blew out her regret in a long stream of air and gathered Charlie tighter to her chest. Things did not always go as planned. That much she knew for certain.

The cabin's interior held the warm glow of a kerosene lantern, just like the ones at her home. Unlike those lanterns, this one had fuel. The interior was familiar and just as she recalled from her Sunrise Ceremony. Each of the cabins had nearly the same style. The inside was all knotty pine with wide plank floors. She remembered that there was a bedroom behind one door and a bathroom behind another. The main room had a table and chairs and a small living area that included a stone fireplace. Someone had lit a fire to chase off the chill.

Upon the opposite wall, a cast-iron stove sat on a brick pad. The table was laden with so much food there was no open place to eat it. The long sideboard held boxes of diapers, baby toys, blankets, baby clothing and even a small bassinet. Beneath the sideboard sat a stroller and car seat. Gifts from her people, she realized.

If she had known about the food, she would have

sent some home with her sisters, for she suspected there was little food there for them. How long until her mother vanished again?

The bedroom door opened and Kacey jumped. Then recognized Colt standing there. The cry that escaped her morphed from fear to joy. She was safe and he was here with her. Kacey began to sob. Colt gathered her up in his arms and she realized the handcuff was no longer clasped to his wrist. He led her to the bedroom.

She had not felt safe in the hospital. Some part of her had feared for Charlie's safety there and she hadn't been able to rest.

Now in the cabin's bedroom, Colt rubbed her back as the tears washed down her cheeks and into the absorbent fabric of his white T-shirt. Her throat ached and she felt bone weary but somehow cleansed when she drew back.

Charlie's forehead wrinkled and he began to cry, as well.

"Let me take him," said Colt.

She passed her baby carefully to him.

Colt took Charlie and rocked him as he had just rocked her. Kacey's arms and back ached from holding the baby since her escape from the hospital. She sank to her seat on the bed. Charlie blinked in a way that foretold of imminent napping. Colt continued to sway, dancing without moving his feet, with her baby in his arms.

Her heart gave a catch at the picture they made. Man and infant, one so strong and one so helpless. She breathed a sigh of contentment mingled with longing. This was what she wanted. But how?

All throughout her captivity, every day and every night, she had been certain that at least one person was searching for her. When she had told the other girls that *they* would come, she had meant Colt. But she'd been wrong. No one had come because no one had searched. They were runaways, lost to their tribe by their own choice. The sorrow grew sharp in her throat like the point of a spear. Their disappearance had been like a rock dropped in the water. Once the ripples ceased, there was no sign of the stone's passing.

Colt carried the sleeping infant to the outer room and returned with him in the bassinet.

"He's had a busy day," said Colt. Then he turned to look at her. "So have you."

She nodded. "Do the police know you are here?"

"Yes. I spoke with Jake. He gave me this." Colt held up a mobile phone for her to see, then set it on the table beside the bassinet. "Even charged it for me."

"What about the FBI? You tackled one of their men."

"I can't leave the reservation."

Her chest tightened. He couldn't leave and she did not want to stay.

"How did you get away from them?"

"They couldn't hold me because they weren't prepared to kill me."

"You've been in here all along?"

"Most of it." Colt sat beside her on the bed.

"Why didn't you come out for the welcoming?"

"I just can't stand so many people. It makes my skin crawl."

"But you'll stay with us?"

"Right here beside you and Charlie."

Kacey swiped at the tears and smiled. "I was so afraid they would take him."

Colt rocked back, bringing her to the mattress with him. Her body throbbed with fatigue and ached from giving birth. But her heart sang and her mind floated as she lay in the warmth and security of his arms.

"Rest now, Kacey. You're safe."

She nodded and nestled closer, dozing, drifting as he stroked her hair. She woke to Charlie's cry. Colt left her to retrieve her newborn. She roused to watch him carry Charlie out of the bedroom and return a moment later with the changing pad. He set this on the dresser and proceeded to change Charlie's diaper and then dress him in a onesie. He moved with more expertise than she did, but Charlie continued to fuss and cry. Her brow wrinkled.

"Where did you learn to do that?" she asked.

"YouTube," he said. "They have Wi-Fi here now. Installed it after the flood. I was in the lodge during your welcome, watching videos on newborn care, and if the information was right, he's still crying because he's hungry."

She held out her arms and accepted her boy. Her breasts ached and milk already flowed before his little mouth latched on to her breast. Charlie was a hungry baby, but after his meal, he was sleepy again.

"He really sleeps a lot," she said, brow knit.

"That's what they do. Eat, sleep and go through diapers." He grinned and her anxiety melted away. This was the old Colt, the sweet boy who was always there with a ready smile and a kind word.

"What about you?" he asked. "You hungry?"

"Starving."

He carried the empty bassinet out to the living area. She followed as soon as Charlie had finished his meal, placing him in the padded carrier. He yawned and closed his eyes.

"Looks comfortable," Colt said.

"They brought me everything I need and more."

They dug into the food provided by their tribe. Kacey was drawn to the sliced roast beef and the hash. She grinned at Colt, who was eating chicken salad. It was almost as she had hoped it would be, before he'd shipped out and she'd been taken.

She cast him a smile. "I'm so glad to be back."

He grinned and it was easy to imagine that he had never changed. But he was different inside now. She sensed it. Were they both so altered that they could not go back?

"Me, too," he said.

"Will you stay here with me?"

He lowered his sandwich. "Yes. But, Kacey, I'm not your best choice. Ty is smarter about this kind of thing and he has Hemi. That canine is the best tracker and guard dog I've ever seen. Jake is a police officer, so he's got a gun and badge and all. Any of the members of Tribal Thunder would stay with you."

"Colt, when my mother took off and we had nothing to eat, the tribe didn't show up. You did. Not your brothers. Not Tribal Thunder. Not protective services. You." She rested a hand on his as the gratitude welled up with the sorrow. Her mouth pressed to a tight line as she forced down the lump in her throat. "You have had my back since second grade when you stepped up for me on the bus. So you are the one I'll trust now."

Colt turned his hand to clasp hers. "I've changed, Kacey."

Her laugh held no mirth and she looked at Charlie sleeping in his bassinet. "We both have. I trust you, Colt. Nothing can change that."

Chapter Nine

Colt dropped his chin to his chest and shook his head as if he could not understand her choice. "Then I'll stay."

She offered him a smile. "Thank you."

Colt reached across the table and took her hand, and the zing of contact darted up her arm toward her chest. "I missed you. When they released me and I made it back, I went to your house."

Her eyes widened. Kaccy withdrew her hand from his. "I didn't know that."

He nodded, his gaze drifting to his hands laced before him and rocking restlessly on the tabletop. "First thing. I spoke to your mother. She said you had run off months ago and hadn't bothered to call. She seemed…"

Kacey could imagine her mother in various states. Needing a fix, after a fix or all business, preparing to leave them again for another long stretch. She swallowed but he said nothing more.

"She thought I'd run," said Kacey. "I'd threatened to more than once."

"No one would have blamed you," he said.

But he knew now that she had not run. Her jaw worked back and forth as if she chewed something tough.

"I didn't understand it. Should have known. You were so excited to start college. I'm ashamed that I believed her. I thought you just couldn't stand to be in that house a minute longer."

She didn't know what to say. Perhaps that she thought he knew her better. "You thought I'd leave my sisters to take care of everything."

"You took care of it alone."

"I had your help, your mother's and Mrs. Trans's."

"You should have had more."

Her gaze drifted away to things unseen. "I've missed the fall semester," she said.

"You'll start in the spring. You can still go."

"With a baby?"

"Why not?"

She realized that he believed she could do it, and that made her think that maybe she could. He'd always given her confidence. She cast him a smile and he returned it. Then she remembered the men who hunted her. Her stomach squeezed and her eyes shifted, glancing toward the locked door. Her smile died as her jaw tightened, bracing herself. There would be no school, no return to normal life, because they were out there. She felt it.

"Well, not for a while, anyway," she said. They shared an uneasy silence. She rubbed the bridge of her nose, thinking of a time he did not want her to go to school.

She'd told him that she'd finally decided the only way to really help her siblings long-term was to get an education. Instead of supporting her choice, he'd joined the Marines and come to her with money to buy them a house. On that day, she had told him she wouldn't be marrying a man who didn't hear her words.

Colt's mom was in failing health, and with his brothers gone, Colt was left to care for May alone. The man she'd found and married, Burt Rope, was loving but not able to cover May's medical bills. The medication costs alone were staggering. So Colt had used his bonus to buy his mom a motorized scooter and banked the rest for her care.

"I wish you had never gone over there," she said.

Colt's expression clouded and his gaze slipped from hers. The tension returned to his shoulders.

"I'm sorry," she said. "I just wish we could both

go back to senior year and… I don't know, run away together."

He nodded, but his chin dipped and his gaze became unfocused. "I'd go this time. But now I wish a lot of things."

"What, Colt?"

"That I could sleep through the night. That I didn't break out in a sweat when I have to get into a car. That I could be around my brothers without wanting to press my hands to my ears and run in the opposite direction. And most of all, I wish I could have been here to protect you."

"I wish I could have been there to protect you, too, Colt."

They stared at each other across the vast expanse of the few feet that separated them. She still wanted to leave. He still wanted to stay. And neither of them would ever be the same again.

"Will you tell me what happened, Kacey?"

Now *her* gaze slid away. "It's hard to talk about."

"I appreciate that."

"Have you spoken to anyone about what happened to you?" she asked.

"Recently. I spoke with Kenshaw. He's getting me a counselor, a man from our tribe who saw action in Afghanistan. We both agreed that living up on the ridge was not making me better. Up until a few days ago, I didn't care. I just wanted to be left alone." He met her gaze. "Then you showed up."

"And now?"

"I want to be there for you, Kacey. That means I have to face what happened and get better."

"Do you think Kenshaw could find me someone to speak to, as well?"

Colt nodded and a smile played at the edges of his full lips. "I'll ask him."

"I didn't talk about it to anyone but the FBI, Colt. I only talked to them because it might help find my friends." She scrubbed her palms over her face, her fingers sliding down her cheeks and away. "They asked me so many questions. I told them all I know. But I never told them how this all made me feel and they never asked. I'm so angry at those men for taking us and so afraid for the girls that they still have. What if they kill them all because of me?" She remembered too late that Colt's entire team was killed. All except him. Her eyes widened and she covered her mouth with one hand. "I'm sorry, Colt."

He swallowed, his Adam's apple bobbing, and he took a moment. "It's hard to live with."

Then he told her about the IED that had destroyed the first Humvee, killing everyone within and disabling his vehicle, wounding two of the five men on his team.

"They had us for three days. They killed the men in my company, one by one." He glanced up at her. "I don't know how you lasted months, Kacey."

She wanted to hear the rest of it, so she did not allow him to draw her away from his story. "How did you survive?"

He laced his hands on his lap and then beat them rhythmically against his thigh. He cleared his throat more than once, but no words came.

She stood and moved her chair to sit beside him and rested a hand over his. He stilled, took a deep breath, then let it go. His voice sounded small now and tight as if he had to force it up from somewhere a long way away.

"They said they were saving me for last. That I was worse than the other infidels because I was brown-skinned like them. They wanted to know what I was."

"Oh, Colt, I'm so sorry."

Colt grimaced. "They'd bring their bodies back one by one and leave them with me. Finally, I was alone with the bodies."

"Jake told me that a SEAL team rescued you."

"They did. But they were too late for my team."

She rubbed his back and then left her arm draped over the tight muscles of his shoulders.

"Too late," she said. "You were the last one out

and I was the first. You know what happened to your men and it was awful. I imagine horrible things. I still have hope, but it lives with the terror of not knowing. I might never know. The hope chases dread like a mockingbird chasing a crow from her nest."

Colt's chin dropped, but he peered up at her from beneath his dark brows and spiky lashes. "It's hard to be the only survivor. I see their faces. In dreams, I hear their voices. I hope they find your friends, Kacey. I don't want you to have to go through this."

"Marta and I had the same due dates. She could have delivered already. What will they do to her then?"

He met her troubled gaze. Neither of them had the answers. Only questions.

Kacey looked in his eyes; saw the pain and the loss. She needed to change the mirror that reflected back to her all that she might suffer. So she kissed him. A light pressing of lips. Colt's eyes closed and his hands slid up her arms to her shoulders. His breathing changed and a hum came from his throat. He deepened the kiss and then she did not think of her friends or his lost comrades because the need took her.

The heat built and her blood pounded. She wanted this, wanted Colt. Kacey pressed herself to him, sitting half across his lap. He dragged her closer until her breasts pushed tight to the firm warm muscles of his torso. The contact was delicious, drawing a moan of pleasure from her.

There was a light tapping on their door. Kacey drew back as Colt released her. She blinked up at him, trying to make sense of the sound. He cursed under his breath and then rose, answering the door. Morgan Strong stood on the porch.

"Kenshaw would like to see you both, if that's possible."

Kenshaw was not only their shaman. He was the head of the medicine society and leader of their warrior sect.

Colt looked to Kacey and she nodded, rising wearily to her feet. She gathered up the carrier where Charlie slept and carried him to the front porch, surprised to see Jack Bear Den standing watch over them. He nodded to her as she passed across the open ground that separated her cabin from the main lodge. There were others watching over them as well, out in the night. Instead of feeling happy at the realization, she thought of all there was to do with the relocation. Surely the detective had other things to do, other cases to solve. The whole thing made her feel guilty to be another drain on their overtaxed resources.

Colt paused outside the lodge, looking at the lights glowing from the windows. She stood with him beneath the stars, holding the plastic handle of the baby carrier. The tension in his body and the change in his breathing drew her attention. She cast him a concerned glance.

"You coming in there with me?" she asked. Kacey didn't know if she could face them alone, but she didn't want to force Colt into a situation where he became anxious.

Colt clenched his teeth, making the muscles in his jaw bulge. Then he nodded. "Yes."

But he didn't move.

"We can leave whenever you say."

He cleared his throat. "Let's get it over with."

She didn't know if it was the gathering or the building that troubled Colt. It didn't matter. He was going for her and she was grateful.

At the lodge, they were greeted by not just Kenshaw and Chief Tinnin, but also FBI field agent Luke Forrest. She hesitated, unsettled to see the FBI here with her protectors.

She stepped back and Kenshaw rose.

"He's not going to take you, Kacey. You're on sovereign land and under the protection of our tribe."

Kacey nodded but did not move forward until Colt placed a hand on her back and gave a little nudge. It surprised her that he was the one to set them in motion. His jaw still clenched, but his eyes were clear and focused as they took the offered seats at the circular council table. Kacey had never been inside the lodge and she looked around at the polished blond logs that supported the high ceiling. The massive fieldstone fireplace sat below the tribal seal, which showed the river, turquoise canyon and a single eagle flying in the blue sky above. The messenger to the great creator, she knew, because this raptor flew higher than all others.

She set Charlie's carrier on the seat beside hers and then took her place, resting her hands on the smooth cool surface of wood. A channel of inlaid turquoise cut through the center of the circular council table and she thought it was intended to resemble the river that gave them life. The wood seemed to radiate a power, and she felt her heartbeat slowing. These men and women were here to help her and protect her baby.

Kacey lifted her head, meeting Kenshaw's gaze. He nodded and gave her an encouraging smile.

"Agent Forrest has told us that you do not remember how you became with child but that you were only seen at our tribe's health clinic. We are therefore initiating an investigation of our clinic. We have hired a new detective. Detective Hood, of the Yavapai Nation, is expected next week and will head this investigation. We thought an outsider might be able to work undercover at the clinic. Also, Detective Hood taking this case will allow Chief Tinnin and Detective Bear Den to continue with their investigation of the eco-extremist group and the supervision of the relocation of our people following the dam breach."

Kenshaw told Kacey that two members of the Wolf Posse had attacked Jake and Lori Redhorse while the couple were protecting the baby they had adopted. Kenshaw set out three photos.

Kacey felt a cold shiver lift the hairs on her body. Her chest went tight, making it difficult to breathe. She knew them. The men were the same pair who had captured her from the high-school athletic fields shortly after her second appointment with the tribe's health clinic. The woman had been in the car holding a gun.

She pushed the photos away and confirmed what they already knew.

"Trey Fields is in federal prison and Minnie Cobb and Earle Glass are on their way there."

He told her that Trey was convicted for endangering a federal officer, Agent Sophia Rivas. Both Minnie Cobb and Earle Glass were in federal custody awaiting trial after twice attempting to snatch Zella's baby.

"I heard about that," said Kacey. "Zella's baby."

She didn't know how to say that the baby in question was white.

"Yes," said Agent Forrest. "Similar situation, only Ms. Colelay is giving up parental rights."

"According to Zella, these two were stalking her for months but avoided capture," said Kenshaw.

Kacey knew who had warned Zella. It was her friend Marta. She knew this because Marta had told her during their captivity that she had told Zella that two bangers were following her. Kacey could only imagine what Zella thought when Marta disappeared and then the two gang members came after her. They'd all been at the clinic the same day. Marta had seen Zella there. But unlike Marta, Kacey did not remember the visit or meeting Zella or anything until the following day. It was like a big black hole.

Before her capture, when she'd told her mother about her memory trouble, her mother said that she wasn't bringing her back to the clinic unless she was bleeding or on fire. Her mother always said that. She'd only taken Kacey in the first place because she needed her college admissions physical. Marta had been there for a high-school sports physical and Kacey had no idea why Zella was there.

"And is her baby safe?" Kacey asked Agent Forrest. She imagined the Russians would want Zella's baby.

"Neither Minnie nor Earle has implicated the gang,

but we feel that neither of them would do something like that without permission at the least. It's more likely that they were under orders. Since their arrest, there have been no further attempts against the infant."

"What about Charlie?" she asked.

"We don't know. That's why we're taking precautions. We have a perimeter and guards posted."

"They killed David SaVala," said Colt, his voice quiet but clear.

"And Bear Den is investigating that death," said Tinnin. "We do think it is related."

"His mobile phone," said Colt. "How did they track that?"

Kacey felt sick to her stomach.

"They'd have to run records for everyone in this area and they'd need the names of the residents up here," said Tinnin.

"That's the kind of information the Wolf Posse could provide," said Agent Forrest.

The Wolf Posse's involvement made the threat greater and more terrible because it now came from within their tribe. The local gang could easily supply the names of everyone who lived up on Turquoise Ridge, including David SaVala.

Another terrible thought came to her. "How did they pick the girls they were going to take?"

Tinnin met her gaze with a look that seemed pitying. "We don't know that yet."

But he had a theory. She'd put money on it. She thought about the others, comparing them to herself. They were all from large families. Those families all had either single parents, like hers, or neglectful parents. Probably both. Most of their folks had occasional run-ins with either the tribal police or child protective services.

Tribal police had been to Kacey's house more than once during those times when her mother left them for days or weeks. She never knew where her mother went, but she always came home with money or drugs or both. Kacey thought of the other girls. She knew from Marta Garcia that protective services had been to the school to speak to her. Brenda Espinoza said that her dad was taken away for hitting her mom. Kacey knew Zella had at least one older sister who had got into trouble very young and Kacey knew that Zella's mom drank.

She made the comparisons and connection. Large troubled families, girls of a certain age. Kacey had considered running away more than once, but to where and what? She was stopped because her sisters and brothers needed her. And she'd had Colt, her rock, until he'd left her to join the service.

She met Tinnin's gaze.

"Did the gang pick us because we wouldn't be missed?" she asked.

Tinnin scrubbed his palm across the stubble on his cheek. "Maybe. You each fit the profile for a runaway."

All the days they had waited for rescue. No one was even looking for them.

Kacey straightened in her seat. Her muscles still ached, but she was determined. It was important that they keep Charlie safe. But it was just as important that they find the missing.

"They think you're looking for them, Chief Tinnin," said Kacey. "They believe that their families and their relatives and their tribe have noticed their disappearance and are searching. They believed me when I said I'd send help. You're telling me that up until I showed up, you had us all listed as runaways."

Tinnin dropped his gaze.

Kacey rose to her feet and rested her palms flat on the table. "You listed us in some database and hoped we got picked up on the streets of Phoenix or wandered on home. Right? No way. They're captives. Taken. And each one of them is pregnant. So we are finding them *now*, before they have their babies and something even worse happens to them."

"FBI is looking for leads at the house you gave us."

"That's not good enough."

"What do you suggest?"

"The clinic. Something happened there," she said. "Something I can't remember."

"Detective Hood will be looking into that connection."

"Next week!" she shouted. "We need to get to the clinic now!"

"What doctor did she see?" asked Colt.

Tinnin looked away.

"I don't remember," said Kacey.

Agent Forrest answered, "Her appointment was with Dr. Kee Redhorse."

Kacey gasped and turned to Colt, who had gone pale. Could Colt's oldest brother have done this to her?

Chapter Ten

Colt looked as if Agent Forrest had punched him. His face went gray and he seemed momentarily stunned. Gradually, he lifted his chin and met Tinnin's stare.

"No," he said. "No way. Not Kee."

"He has taken on substantial debt," said Tinnin. Both his tone and his eyes reflected sympathy. His words, however, cut again.

"Lots of people have debt," Kacey said, coming to Kee's defense. She knew that Colt's oldest brother was both an example and a father to him. She also knew that when Kee left for college, Colt missed him terribly.

"What about Ty?" she asked. "He's a member of the Wolf Posse. Isn't he more likely to be involved?" Only after the words were spoken did she realize what she had done. Implicating his other older brother did not make things better. She gasped and pressed a hand to her mouth.

Colt's jaw muscles bunched and he flinched, telling her without words how much her comment hurt him.

"We are aware," Tinnin said, "and are exploring his possible involvement."

So they were looking at Ty and Kee.

Kacey slipped her hand from her mouth and whispered an apology to Colt. He cast her a cutting glance and then looked away.

"We request that you two stay here on this property so Tribal Thunder can keep you safe. We also ask that you limit your interaction with both Kee and Ty," said Tinnin.

"Limit it to what?" asked Colt.

"Zero," said Agent Forrest.

Colt looked from one man to the other.

For how long? she wanted to ask. She had escaped her captors and found safety, but for Colt, this was a different type of prison. He did not like being confined and she suspected the size of the property made little difference.

As for herself, she was relieved that Charlie was safe. But it sat badly that she was free when her friends were still captives. What if their captors had done something worse than move them? What if they had been killed because of her? Or had their babies taken?

The theory of growing fetal tissue rose in her mind like a waking nightmare, and her gaze cut to her sleeping baby.

She couldn't live with that. They had to find them.

"Any progress on locating Brenda, Marta and Maggie?" she asked.

Tinnin sighed and pushed his gum to his cheek before answering. "FBI is still processing evidence, but there is nothing new." His jaw worked the gum between his molars. "Listen, you've had a long day. We'll check back in the morning." His gaze flicked to Colt. "If you plan to stay, we've got you in the cabin beside Kacey's."

But the implication was clear. Tinnin didn't expect Colt to remain or perhaps he did not want him to stay. In fact, with the investigation now centering on both Kee and Ty Redhorse, it was very possible that the chief would prefer that Colt leave.

Colt glanced to her. She reached out and clasped his hand.

"Stay," she said on a release of breath.

His nod was tight. Then he turned to Tinnin. "I come and go as I like." It wasn't a request.

Tinnin lifted his dark brows, turning the skin on his forehead into a road map of horizontal furrows.

"You need to stay on-site," said Tinnin.

Colt said nothing to this. Forrest and Tinnin exchanged a side glance. Forrest arched a brow. One more Redhorse to add to their list of suspects, she thought. Or just a loose cannon? Colt's mutiny meant more work for a police force already stretched past its limits. But she knew that neither of these men nor Tribal Thunder could keep Colt here if he did not wish to stay. Colt was like a shadow in the woods.

He stepped around the table to face off against Agent Forrest, and his hands squeezed into fists. Nothing good had ever come from two men posturing like that, she knew.

She lifted Charlie from his bassinet and stepped up beside Colt, pressing her shoulder to his. He tore his gaze away from the field agent and glanced first at her and then at Charlie, who slept with his mouth open. Kacey didn't ask; she just placed Charlie in Colt's arms.

Forrest stepped back as if she'd handed Colt a live grenade. It seemed she had found the men's weakness. Babies made many men uncomfortable. But not Colt. He cradled Charlie's head as her baby nestled against his shoulder.

"We need to get him to bed," she said. Of course, Charlie didn't care if he slept in a bassinet, his mother's arms or in a cradleboard. But Colt needed to be free of these two men.

He cast the two tribal police officers one last look,

his mouth going tight. Then he turned away, still cradling Charlie.

Kacey lifted the empty bassinet and faced Tinnin, Forrest and Little Falcon.

"Good night, gentlemen," she said to them. "I thank you for providing us a safe place. I wish my friends had the same."

Kacey followed Colt out across the wide-open ground that separated the main lodge from the row of cabins along the river. The trees that lined the shore provided glimpses of the silver ribbon of water moving swiftly along. Too swiftly, she realized now that the dam no longer controlled the flow of water.

She gazed up at the deep dark skies alive with bright sparks of light. The wind brushed over her skin and she closed her eyes to savor the beauty and the peace as she gave thanks to the One Who Lives Above.

She was free. Just days ago, she had fled for her life and now she was here on her tribe's lands. It seemed impossible. She opened her eyes to look at the heavens and found the star that does not walk around, the North Star. It was there as it had been every night of her life. It had not changed in her absence. Stars were constant. Would any of her friends ever see the night sky again? The tears came then, streaking down her cheeks.

When she lowered her gaze from the night sky, it was to find Colt staring back at her. He used the warm pad of his thumb to wipe her cheeks dry.

"It's so beautiful here." She swallowed against the lump that rose suddenly in her throat.

"Yes." He took her elbow and gave a squeeze.

"I wish… I wish my friends could see this."

His hand stroked up and down her arm and then rubbed across her back.

"I'm afraid what they'll do to them because of me."

His face was serious and he offered no false hope. He had friends as well, comrades who would never see the night sky or anything else again. He understood and did not minimize her fears with words. Instead, he gave comfort a different way by wrapping his free arm around her shoulders and ushering her forward to the cabin.

"I'm sorry for what I said about Ty," she whispered.

He didn't answer as they crossed the open ground and she thought he did not hear her. When they reached the porch, he turned to face her.

"It was a natural conclusion," he said. "He was in the gang. But he's not in it anymore."

"My mother says no one ever leaves the Posse."

What she had actually said was that the only way out was dying. But Kacey wouldn't say that aloud.

"Maybe so," he said. "Let's get Charlie inside. Cold out here."

Every evening was cold in the fall. With no cloud cover, the earth cooled rapidly.

Colt held open the door and she stepped inside.

Charlie roused when Colt handed him back to her. Colt used a match to light the lantern and set about rousing the fire in the cast-iron stove to chase off the evening chill.

As he continued to feed the growing fire with sticks of kindling and then logs, she fed Charlie. She tried not to feel guilty that she sat in the comfortable cabin or wonder where her friends were right now. The skin of her naked breast puckered at exposure to the cool air, but gradually the fire's heat reached her. By the time she switched Charlie to her opposite breast, she was humming.

She did not forget her pain or her promise, but her baby needed her. Could she risk something else happening to her? What would happen to Charlie then? Her mother was incapable of caring for him. Kacey had been in the tribe's foster-care system at various times. Sometimes she stayed with Colt's mother and helped look after Colt's sister, Abbie.

Many foster families here were good, but many

were little better than the family from which she had been taken. She didn't want that for Charlie.

She looked down at the sweet face of her child. He stared up at her from deep blue eyes. The irises hinted that his eyes would be dark one day. His skin was lighter than her little brothers' had been, and the fuzz on his head was a soft brown. She stroked his perfect head.

Not hers, but still hers.

"I don't care about DNA and genetics," she said to Charlie. "They took my freedom, so I'll take you. Fair exchange. You're mine."

She felt Colt staring at her. She lifted her gaze from her baby to him and smiled.

"Do you think they will let me keep him?" she asked.

"The tribe, yes. The FBI, I don't know."

"He's not evidence. He's a baby. My baby."

"As long as you stay here, they have no power to take Charlie."

"Are you staying here tonight?" she asked.

"Maybe not in the cabin. I like to sleep outside."

"I could open the windows."

"Won't it be too cold for Charlie?"

"No. We have blankets and someone left a wolf pelt."

"You want me to stay?" he asked.

She nodded. "I feel safe when you are here."

He stood and used one finger to rub at the corner of his eye. "You heard them, right? About Kee and Ty."

"But your brother Jake is a member of the police force and he's a member of Tribal Thunder."

"Do you think it's possible, what they suspect?" he asked.

She lifted one shoulder and then let it drop.

"Do you remember who saw you at the clinic?" he asked.

"Which time?"

"The first."

"January sometime. I know that much." Kacey shook her head. "I told you. I don't even remember going to the clinic or much of the following day. It's like I just jumped over them."

"I wish I could forget, sometimes."

She could understand that.

"Do you think you can't remember because of the trauma?" he asked.

"No. None of us could remember." Kacey didn't think she was blocking out her experience. The other explanation she refused to say aloud.

"Could you have been drugged?" he asked.

She shrugged. "I don't know." But she suspected.

"They might have used that date-rape drug," said Colt.

She lifted her brows and prepared to agree and instead shook her head. "I don't think so."

"You don't remember," he said. "What about your mother?"

At the mention of her mother an instant knot gripped the muscles between her shoulder blades. "What about her?"

"She might remember who saw you."

Kacey snorted. "She only drove me because she needed the car. She told me that she didn't go in for the physical with me, just dropped me off at the door." Like a stray cat outside an animal shelter, Kacey thought. But that was better than the alternative. "Then they called for a follow-up in February. Mom was annoyed. The woman who called said there was a problem with my blood sample and they had to redo it."

"They found something?" he asked.

"Lost it, was what my mother said."

"Who did she speak to?" he asked.

"I don't know. I found the note on the counter telling me to drop in. No appointment necessary. I did and they took blood and urine. I have no trouble remembering that appointment. That was February 20th. They took me on February 22nd."

"You remember that?"

"Every detail."

Chapter Eleven

Colt listened as Kacey described being snatched off the road after leaving the late school bus after volleyball practice during the half-mile walk to her home. It had been dark, even though it was well before six in the evening and she had been alone. Her brothers, still in elementary school, took an earlier bus, and her sisters, Jackie, Winnie and Shirley, did not play sports. No one else used that stop.

It had been Kacey and two male attackers. She knew their names or at least the names that they called each other. Earle and Trey. She had seen them around. Minnie had been there, too, in the car. Kenshaw had shown her their photos and said they were all members of the Wolf Posse. Trey was in prison and Minnie and Earle were in custody.

She could not find it in her heart to be sorry. From each girl's description, Marta had been taken by Minnie and Trey, Brenda by Earle alone and Maggie by someone else. Kacey hoped to God it had not been Ty.

Kacey knew her abductors were all gang members because they wore yellow and black, the Posse's colors. They had simply lifted her off the ground and thrown her into the van. She had lost one of her sneakers; evidence, she had thought at the time. A clue to lead someone to her. Now she knew better.

Once they were inside the van, Minnie pointed the pistol at her. Earle and Trey used duct tape on her wrists, ankles and mouth. They threw her backpack in the back with her. They carried her from the van and into the house. All the while, she had been wiggling like a fly wrapped in a spider's web with just as much chance of escape.

In the house, she saw the Russians for the first time. They paid Trey in cash. When the Russians had taken her to the basement, she was certain she would never again come back up those dusty wooden stairs. She shivered, the terror fresh as raw meat.

"You told Tribal this?" Colt asked.

She nodded. "Took them to the house, too. You know, every episode of that FBI show flashed in my mind. The body, the evidence, but not what the victim suffered," she said. "Not the days and weeks locked in a basement."

Colt took her hand. She wondered if his own capture was roaring through his mind, because his forehead glistened with perspiration.

"After they left me there, still taped up like a carpet, Marta appeared."

Marta had been taken at the beginning of February and had been alone in that basement for nineteen days. She had released Kacey, told her what little she knew.

"We thought they were crazy, telling us to eat and take care of the baby. But then Marta started throwing up."

She told him of living in the basement for months. And how they kept a calendar on the floor, scratching in the days. That was how she knew that Brenda Espinoza came in May and Maggie Kesselman arrived in late September.

"Do you think they moved them?" he asked. The implication was clear. If they were not moved, then they were dead.

"I hope so. None of them cared about us. But they sure cared about the babies. Kept us fed. Gave us vitamins. Let us wash and gave us each a mattress and a wool blanket. They were scratchy but warm. This was about the babies."

He thought of Charlie and wondered where he would be now if Kacey had not escaped. "Do you know anything about the people who are the genetic parents? Do they know?"

She rubbed her brow with the heel of her hand, then let it drop. "I don't know anything about them. I have spent a lot of time thinking about them. All I know is what Agent Forrest told me during our first interview. The FBI lab report said that Charlie is Caucasian and Asian."

"No. He's Turquoise Canyon Apache," Colt said.

She smiled at that. Her heart twisted in her chest at the sweetness of his smile and the sorrow in his eyes.

"Well, you're safe now with Tribal Thunder protecting you."

"They still want Charlie," she said.

"Too bad. Because they won't get him," said Colt.

She smiled and glanced back to where her baby slept. In the lamplight, she could see his mouth working as if he sucked, even in slumber, with his hands raised beside his head, perfect fingers curled into tiny palms.

Colt stepped up behind her, his arms slipping around her waist and his mouth descending to her neck. They had told her at the hospital that she should not sleep with a man for two weeks or more. That her body needed time to heal. But her body did not know or care about rules. And her heart did not know caution, for her heart sped, galloping along in anticipation. She lifted her hand to stroke his head, drawing his sweet mouth closer to the juncture of her neck and shoulder.

She turned in his arms and he lifted his head, meeting her gaze. Her brows rose as she pressed their hips together.

Colt stiffened as her stomach met the hard ridge of male flesh.

"It's too soon," he said.

"For that," she said. "Do you remember all the times we went to the river?"

His eyes rounded. Kacey had kept her virginity. She and Colt had never had sex. But they had learned how to reach their pleasure without intercourse.

Colt's smile was slow and languid. She stroked his arousal.

"I remember," he said. "Everything."

They moved into the bedroom, Colt carrying the lantern and Kacey carrying Charlie. He left the door open to let the heat from the stove follow them.

She wrapped Charlie in the wolf pelt and laid him back in the crib beside the bed. He did not even wake as she moved him.

Colt waited for her on the bed. He'd drawn back the covers so that only half of the bright red, green and black of the Navajo-patterned blanket was visible under the white sheets. The lantern now sat on a shelf above the bed, made for that purpose.

She sat on the opposite side and turned to look past the two pillows and the wide expanse of linen at Colt. He offered her a wicked smile.

Kacey removed her shoes and socks, but nothing else, before lying on the bed. She rolled to her back as he settled to his side. They met in the middle.

His kisses moved from her neck to her ear, sending delight shivering over her skin. Kacey caressed his head, gliding her fingers through the loose satin of his long hair before entwining her fingers behind his neck and pulling him down until his body pressed tight to hers. All the while, he continued to score the flesh at her neck with his sharp teeth. His fingers danced feather light across her hip and stomach until she could not stand having their clothing separating them.

He helped draw away her blouse, kissing the skin he revealed as he stripped her out of her jeans. When he finally climbed back up to lie beside her, Kacey was breathless and dressed only in a bra and panties. Her body hummed with anticipation as he turned away, stood and shucked out of his jeans, flannel shirt and undershirt.

When he returned to her, she reached for him, using her hand to do what her body was not ready for as he slipped a hand beneath her panties and caressed the wet wanting flesh at the junction of her thighs. His fingers moved expertly, parting her and finding the bud of needy flesh. He stroked as he rocked against her hip.

"I missed this," he said.

"I missed us," she said.

His gaze locked to hers and she saw the tension build. But he continued with long, even strokes as he teased and rubbed her toward her release. Her head dropped back and her breathing changed. He moved faster, his hot breath blasting against her throat. She arched up to meet her release, her body stiffening a moment before the wave of pleasure broke within her. She gasped and then gave a hum of pleasure. He kissed her then, pressing her back to the pillows as he cried out, his release pulsing in her hand.

His body went slack and he dropped to her side. His heavy arm fell across her middle. She clasped hold with both hands and rolled toward him until their foreheads touched.

"All you all right?" he asked.

The muscles that had responded to her need now ached. But she smiled. "I'm fine."

He rolled away and returned with a small damp towel for her and one for him. When she felt clean again, the exhaustion returned. She changed Charlie's diaper and saw him settled before crawling into the nightie someone had provided for her and then returning to the bed. Colt appeared a moment later dressed in low-slung sweatpants that gave her a view of his chest and abdomen that she would never forget.

"You're staying?"

He smiled. "I don't feel trapped when I'm with you. It seems natural to be here." He rubbed the back of his neck. "I haven't talked so much since I came home."

"I missed talking to you," she said. "Sometimes, while I was in that basement, I would imagine what you would say to me."

His hand dropped to his side and he looked bereft. "What did you imagine I'd say?"

She smiled. "'Be brave.'" She looked away, fluffing the pillows. She did not tell him the rest. *Be brave. I'll find you.* Even though he'd not been looking for her. Knowing that hurt her down in the place below her heart.

He slipped in beside her and stroked her hair away from her face.

"We never did this before," he said.

"Yes, we have."

"No, not this. I never had a chance to sleep beside you afterward, Kacey. I always had you home before it got too late."

As if the time of day had anything to do with what teens wanted to do when they were alone.

"That's true." She glanced toward the window. "They'll all know you slept here."

"I'll leave if that is what you'd like."

She gripped his hand. "No. I need you here."

"I don't sleep much," Colt admitted.

She cast him a smile. "Maybe tonight will be different."

Colt reached up and snuffed the lantern. It glowed a familiar eerie orange ghost light before fading so slowly she was not sure she saw the moment it went out.

Colt moved close and gathered her up against the welcome heat of his body. He pressed a kiss to her temple and then laid his head down on the pillow beside hers. She rested as his breathing fanned her forehead, feeling his body relax as he drifted to sleep.

She closed her eyes and gnawed at her lower lip. She was safe here. Kacey knew it. And that was exactly the problem.

The food and the warmth and the comfort of the bed all offended her. Why were they not all out looking for Maggie and Marta and Brenda?

They were all out there waiting, huddled together, watching their bellies grow bigger day by day. At least she hoped they were still captives, because the alternative was too terrible to consider.

Kacey had promised them that she'd send help, and just like everyone else, she had failed them.

Kacey did not sleep well. Between her dreams of the various horrors that might be befalling her friends and the needs of a newborn, she spent as much time in the bedroom as she did in the outer living space. When she finally did fall deeply asleep in the hours between night and dawn, it was to visions of rescue. Only this time when she dreamed of her friends' release, Kacey was with them.

All this time, she had been waiting for someone to find her, to rescue them. She woke with a start, her eyes flashing open. Kacey blinked in the gray predawn light that made it possible for her to see nothing and everything all at once. She held the dream in her mind, trapping it in her conscious thoughts.

She knew what she must do. The idea was simple and terrible and dangerous. But it might work.

Chapter Twelve

Colt's eyes opened and he took in his surroundings.
The cabin was familiar but not his own. He knew
where he was, but the light from the window told
him this was morning.

And that was impossible.

It would mean that he had slept through the entire
night. He had not done that since before his capture.
In a moment, he knew the reason. The weight of the
body next to him on the mattress was the answer.
Kacey slept at his side. She was safe, so he was safe.
Nothing would touch them here. He let his eyes drift
closed and then he realized what had woken him.
Kacey's breathing was wrong. He turned to look at
her as she stared straight up to the ceiling.

Had she been dreaming—rushing sloth-like from
the grip of some unseen terror? Colt knew nightmares
intimately. All types. He had the ghosts of his com-

rades to dog him. She had the ghosts of her friends haunting her.

He took her in his arms and dragged her close. He lifted his head to look at her. She lay rigid as a corpse with eyes wide open. Whatever frightened Kacey, it was no nightmare.

"Kacey?"

She didn't answer or even seem to hear him. Now his heart was pounding.

KACEY LIFTED HER hand over her mouth because the idea scared her so much. Her eyes went wide as the pieces tumbled against each other like river rocks rolling in floodwaters. None of the law-enforcement personnel could find the missing women because none of them were willing to use the one thing that might bring her captors out of the shadows.

Was she willing?

Someone had wanted Zella's baby badly enough to send Minnie Cobb and Earle Glass after her. That gave Kacey the lure, something the Russians wanted and the gang wanted. The FBI and tribal police had both given her the place, the clinic. Somehow someone there had notified the gang when Zella's baby arrived. Would they do so again?

She had the who and the where. All that was left was when and how.

Kacey would never use her child as bait. But she would use herself. She knew the risks. Knew them precisely. But that would not stop her.

She had promised her friends that she would send help and she had failed. Now she saw a way to keep her promise.

"Kacey?" Colt's voice held a mix of concern and uncertainty.

She turned to meet his dark eyes to find him watching her with knit brow.

"Didn't you hear me?"

She shook her head. Had he spoken to her?

"What's wrong?" he asked.

It was hard to say it aloud. Somehow she did. "I have to let my captors catch me."

His nostrils flared and he pushed himself up to one elbow, so that he loomed over her. "No."

It wasn't up to him. Perhaps he knew that, which was why he looked so fierce.

She sat up in bed and tucked a leg up underneath herself as she turned to face him. "Tribal police can't find them without me."

"They'll have to."

"It's taking too long."

"Be patient. Give the force time to work."

"Time?" She made a strangled sound that combined the gnashing of teeth and the growl of a beast. "How can you say that to me?"

"The FBI is working leads. Agent Forrest said so. It's only been a few days."

"You were only captive a few days."

His face contorted as if she had struck him and she knew her verbal blow had hit its mark.

Colt opened his mouth to argue and then shut it again.

"Marta is due any day," said Kacey. "She might already have had her baby. What happens to her then? I'll tell you what will happen. I'll repeat what I heard them say about me. 'Sell her or dump her.' You understand? Once the baby comes, the Russians either sell her into slavery or kill her. That's what is happening right now."

Colt's brow descended and his dark eyes turned to flint. "I don't care what happens to her. I care what happens to you."

"Well, if you knew that any day, any hour those evil men would kill me or sell me, what then? Would you still not care?"

He stared belligerently at her, unrelenting. She slipped from her side of the bed. The pine planks chilled her bare feet as she gathered one of his clenched fists in her two hands.

"Colt, what if your comrades were still in captivity? What would you be prepared to do to free them?"

His eyes shifted, darting away as he looked at something far off.

"Anything," he whispered.

She smiled. He understood.

He flicked his gaze back to her. "But you are not a soldier, Kacey. You are a mother with a child. What happens to Charlie if you don't come back? Will you leave him for your mother to raise?"

Colt was fighting back, hitting her in her most vulnerable place.

Kacey swallowed at the lump that rose in her throat, but it remained lodged like a shard of glass. She dropped his hand and stepped back. He followed her, sliding across the empty bed and coming to stand before her.

She turned her back. Colt knew exactly how bad her home life had been, because he'd seen it and because she'd told him. It was one of many reasons that everyone assumed she had run. Why would anyone stay in such a home a minute longer than necessary?

Colt took her in his arms, drawing her back

against the strength and heat of his body. His arms wrapped her in a warm embrace, and his breath fanned her neck. She gave in to the perfect fit and the compelling heat of him.

His breath whispered over her skin, bringing a delicious shiver.

"I came home for you, Kacey. I only just found you again and now you're asking me to risk losing you, too? I won't."

Somehow she mustered the courage to step away. She faced him, meeting his angry stare. He was going to protect her with or without her permission. She narrowed her eyes, astonished at how quickly they had gone from lovers to opponents. Well, for her friends, she would fight even him.

He seemed to know her mind, because his brows fell low and menacing over his dark eyes. "I'll lock you up myself."

She exhaled, centering herself and finding her strength, knowing she would need both. Then she turned away, separating from him, but he clasped her arm, tethering her with a firm grip.

"Don't leave me, Kacey. Don't do this."

"Let me go, Colt."

"I can't."

She met his gaze with a defiant stare. If she had to hurt him to save her friends, so be it.

"You did once," she said.

His hand slipped away as his eyes widened. His jaw dropped and then snapped shut as he whirled, heading toward the outer room.

She somehow resisted the urge to go after him by picturing Marta giving birth in the room with silver stirrups. She saw to Charlie's needs as Colt stomped around between the woodpile and the stove.

She retreated to the bathroom to clean up. It was Wednesday, and with each day, each hour, as Marta, Brenda and Maggie grew heavier, their chances of rescue grew slimmer.

After showering, she dressed in clothing provided by her tribe. They were nicer than anything she had ever had in her closet.

She stepped out to the bedroom and gathered Charlie in her arms and fed her baby.

Colt returned as she was snapping the onesie onto Charlie's kicking legs.

"I brought breakfast," he said and retreated.

She followed him to the outer room. The stove warmed the room, and the air held the aroma of bacon. She set Charlie in his carrier in the seat beside her and then seated herself. Colt set a plate before her with crisp bacon, fried eggs flecked with black pepper, charred toast and browned potatoes mixed with onions and bits of red bell peppers.

"So what's your plan?" he asked.

"Do you think Ty could get word to the Wolf Posse about where I am?"

Colt stopped eating. "He's managing to keep those bangers at arm's length. Why would you drag him into this?"

"I need the Russians to know where I am."

"You think the Wolf Posse doesn't know exactly where you are? They know, so the Russians know."

She realized that was true, and with that recognition came another. "I'm too well guarded for them to reach me."

"Exactly. Isn't that why we're here?" He motioned to the cabin, safe in the tribal headquarters and surrounded by the guardians of her people.

"I have to leave."

"With Charlie?"

The cold flash of terror of that possibility caused a physical pain to tear across her middle. Her denial was quick. "No. He stays here, where he is safe."

"They don't want you. They want him."

"I know that."

"Do you think the tribe will protect this child if you leave?"

"'This child'? What are you saying?"

"He's your baby if you say so. Your say-so also makes him Apache. But without you here—"

"He's Apache," she insisted.

"Without you to claim him, he would need to be adopted by another member of our tribe. These men and women are risking their lives to protect you, Kacey. But who would adopt a child who endangers their lives?"

This part made Kacey's insides hurt. But she pressed on, crossing her arms over her middle and hunching as if expecting a kick. "Your brother Jake and his new wife, Lori, are both Tribal Thunder and they have a newborn. Zella's baby."

"Yes."

"Well, how is it that their baby is safe?"

"Zella Colelay was not a captive."

"But her baby came to her in the same way. The FBI told us that members of the Wolf Posse tried to capture the baby Jake and Lori are adopting. So why doesn't the Wolf Posse want her anymore?"

Colt shook his head. "I have no answer."

Kacey needed to protect Charlie and she needed to help her friends. She was torn. "Would Ty know?"

His gaze cast down and he did not answer for a long stretch. Finally he spit one word. "Probably."

"Would Lori take Charlie?" she asked.

He was scowling. "Lot to ask."

"She swore an oath to protect," she said.

He grimaced. But he did not say that they protected members of the tribe. She counted Charlie as one of them and she believed Colt did, as well. But many might think otherwise. Charlie had no tribal blood and everyone knew it. Adopted children were accepted by her people. But if no one would adopt Charlie, what would happen to him? And who would be brave enough to adopt him, especially if he brought danger to their tribe?

"Taking Charlie would jeopardize their little girl," he said.

The Turquoise Canyon people were only just rising after the attack by the eco-extremists. People had to evacuate from their homes and move to temporary housing. Now she returned with the Russian mob on her tail. It was terrible timing.

"I'll call Jake and ask him to stop by."

He made the call and reached his brother. He told Jake that he was putting the call on speaker.

"I was just going to call you," said Jake. "I have some bad news."

Kacey braced for word that her friends had been killed.

"We're missing another girl."

"What? Who?" asked Colt.

"Louisa Tah."

Colt glanced at her and she shook her head. She did not know Louisa.

"School reported Louisa missing on Monday, October 2nd," said Jake.

Six days before Kacey had escaped, another girl had been taken.

"Missing. Ran or taken?" asked Colt.

"We don't know."

"You just finding out now?"

"No. We've been investigating," said Jake. "We got word on Monday from the school of Louisa's absence because they could not reach the mother. We made contact and her mom thought that Louisa would turn up. She hasn't. Her mother is hazy on when she last saw her daughter, so exactly when Louisa disappeared is unknown. Louisa was in school Friday and missing on Monday."

Louisa had been gone for days before her absence had been reported. Kacey's heart squeezed. She already knew Louisa without knowing her. All she needed to do was look in a mirror. No one had missed her.

"Yeah. She's sixteen. Lives in Koun'nde. Ran with the gang but never made it to initiation."

Colt set down the phone on the table and gripped

the arms of his chair. Kacey found she'd made a fist of her right hand and was pressing it to her mouth.

"After the school reported her truant, one of our guys tracked down her grandmother, because Louisa stays there sometimes, but she wasn't there. I did the interview with mom. Mrs. Tah was intoxicated when I got there Monday afternoon. I called protective services and waited for them to arrive. Mrs. Tah has three other children all under the age of six."

Kacey closed her eyes against the dread.

"Anyway. Both mom and grandmom thought Louisa was staying with the other one."

"That's terrible," said Colt, his eyes on Kacey now.

She shivered as if the temperature in the room had dropped.

"Was she seen at the clinic?" asked Kacey.

"Checking," said Jake. "Listen, it's an active investigation. I just called to ask if Kacey saw her."

"Saw her when?"

"During her captivity."

"No," she said.

"Okay, Lori and I are on our way over to the tribal grounds now. We'll be there in a few minutes," said Jake.

"Good. We have something else to discuss with you and Lori. See you soon," said Colt.

"'Bye for now." Jake disconnected.

The silence stretched.

"They didn't bring a mattress," she said.

"What?"

"The day before they arrive they bring a mattress. They didn't bring one."

"Kacey, this isn't your fault. No one expects you to go out there like the Lone Ranger."

"Call Ty."

He met her stare with a look of frustration. He pushed the phone at her. "You call him."

She lifted the phone in a trembling hand. Her hands shook so hard it was difficult to even bring the screen to life.

"What if you don't come back?" he asked.

She had once asked him the same thing after she learned that he had enlisted.

"I have to do this." It was what he had said to her.

"Call Forrest. At least tell him what you're planning."

"They'll stop me. I need your help, Colt."

"I'm not helping you get Ty arrested or yourself killed."

"Will you take Charlie?"

"What?"

"You're a member of the tribe. Full blood. You can adopt him."

"They won't let me adopt a baby. Psych discharge, remember? They think I'm loco, baying at the moon."

"You could do it."

He frowned, his lips pressed thin. His answer ground between clenched teeth. "No."

Was that the truth or was it just a way to keep her here?

"I have to help them. I promised."

He rose to his feet, his face red and his breathing ragged. "How will getting killed help them?"

She reached for him and he backed away, arms raised as if to say he would have no part in this. "You are not going," he stated.

She lowered her chin. He held her gaze and saw no wavering in her conviction.

He lifted his hands in surrender. "All right. I'll talk to Ty. I can't talk about this on the phone. I have to go to him."

"Thank you."

He stormed out of the cabin without his phone. She scooped up the baby carrier and the phone, but by the time she reached the porch, Colt was already on his brother's motorcycle, pulling out.

She watched him go, disappearing from sight in the tunnel of pines that led in and out of the tribe's gathering place. She slipped his phone into her pocket and then paused. The sound of an engine kept her there on the porch, listening. It idled and she thought that he might have changed his mind and turned around. But a few minutes later, two vehicles pulled in.

The first was a silver F-150 pickup. She recognized the driver. It was Jake Redhorse, she realized. He must have passed Colt on his way in. What had Colt told his brother, the newest member of the tribal police force?

As the truck turned toward the lodge, she more clearly saw the second vehicle, a dust-covered black Ford Escort, and the driver, Jake's new wife, Lori.

Kacey watched Jake pull up before the lodge. The Escort parked beside his truck. He emerged first.

Colt's next oldest brother resembled his mother much more than Colt did, with a heavier brow and fuller mouth. He was out of uniform today, wearing jeans and a long-sleeved shirt. He spotted her and waved as he rounded the truck, opening the door of the dusty compact car.

Lori emerged from the car dressed in blue scrubs and a top covered with pastel graphics of children's toys. Her hair was tied in a bun and she wore her hospital identification tag around her neck. Lori had a regal look about her and clear light brown skin with coral undertones. Jake's new wife paused to open her window, likely to prevent the car's interior from heating up.

The implications of the two vehicles and Lori's attire struck Kacey, and her breath caught. Jake was coming to work with Tribal Thunder, and Lori was headed to work…at the clinic.

Kacey lifted Charlie from his carrier and crossed to them. What had Colt told his brother?

"WE JUST SAW COLT," said Lori. "He's finally going to see his mama."

Kacey blinked at the lie. He had told her he was going to see Ty. Should she tell Jake where Colt was really heading?

Jake regarded her and she tried to keep from squirming.

"How did you manage that?" he asked.

Colt had lied to someone. He was going to see either Ty or his mother, but not both.

"Not sure," she said. Colt was on a mission. She just didn't know which one. "Any word on Louisa?" she asked.

Jake shook his head.

"My friends?" she asked.

"Not that I've heard."

Lori stepped up on the porch and asked to see Charlie. Kacey hesitated only a moment before turning him over. Lori was a member of Tribal Thunder and a prenatal nurse. But she worked at the clinic. And that was where this all had started.

"You heading to work?" asked Kacey.

"Yes, in a few minutes. I just need to check my schedule here first."

Kacey recognized that this output of time and effort could not go on indefinitely. If they did not catch the men responsible, these men and women would eventually need to return to their lives.

The trunk of Lori's Escort was covered with bumper stickers urging you to donate blood, kiss a nurse and have Native Pride. Kacey stared at the vehicle and then her gaze flicked to the open front window.

She lifted her gaze to find Lori fussing over Charlie. The neonatal nurse held her baby with confidence. Her newborn must have sensed it, for he did not fuss as he relaxed against Lori's chest and shoulder.

"How are you feeling?" asked Lori.

Kacey answered that and several other medical

questions before Lori was satisfied. Kacey turned to Jake.

"How is it that no one is after your baby girl?" asked Kacey.

Jake glanced at Lori, who nodded.

"Tell her."

"I made a deal with Faras Pike."

That was the leader of the tribe's gang, Kacey knew.

"Told him that we're expecting a new detective who could be assigned to gang violence or the eco-extremists case based on what Faras decided to do about my little girl."

"A threat? And that stopped it?" Kacey asked. It seemed too convenient. Surely the threat Faras received over *not* delivering the infant was worse. Something didn't seem quite right about his story.

"I also spoke to Ty."

Now, that she believed. It was not threats that convinced Faras to withdraw but something Ty had said or offered. What? she wondered. A deal? A favor? Then the other shoe dropped.

Kacey could not prevent the gasp. If Ty worked a deal with Faras, then he owed Faras.

What was that favor? Was it Charlie? She resisted the urge to snatch Charlie back. She'd sent Colt to Ty, and Ty might very well be working for Faras. Suddenly all the warmth left the day and she shivered.

Jake had been leaning a hip against the rear fender of his wife's compact car. But now he came upright and his arms dropped to his sides.

"Kacey? What's wrong?"

"I asked Colt to speak to Ty about Charlie."

Now Jake seemed alarmed, judging from the way he swung his gaze about in the direction Colt had disappeared. "Is that where Colt went?"

"He said so, yes. But I don't know."

Jake pinched the bridge of his nose with his thumb and index finger. "I already spoke to Ty. He said there was nothing he could do."

She wondered if the grief showed on her face. The possibility that Colt might persuade Ty to help protect Charlie had kept her hope alive. It died now with the silence of a snuffed candle as her convictions hardened to flint.

"Can he help find Marta and Brenda, Louisa and Maggie?"

Jake's hand moved to the back of his neck. "He's not in the gang, Kacey. They don't tell him things like that. He fixes their cars and trucks. He looks the other way on things he shouldn't and tries to walk a very fine line between them and us. I'm not asking him to do something that I know can get him killed."

She thought that he might already have done that. "I understand." She opened her arms for Charlie, and Lori handed him back.

"I've got to call Colt," said Jake.

Kacey slipped her hand into her pocket and flipped Colt's phone to mute just a moment before it began to vibrate with Jake's call.

"I'll see you two later," said Jake, his phone to his ear as he marched off. Lori looked after her husband as Kacey retreated a step toward her cabin.

Kacey directed her next comments to Charlie. "Nap time for you, mister."

Somehow she held her smile until after she was walking away.

Chapter Thirteen

Kacey turned at the porch and watched Jake and Lori make their way to the main lodge. Jake still pressed his phone to his ear. When they disappeared inside, Kacey's knees gave way and she sat hard on the porch of the little cabin. The weight of her decision pressed down on her and she could not rise. She thought of all the ways her idea could fail, and the list was long. Then she thought of the seconds she had to make her decision ticking away. Finally, she imagined what might happen, the release of her friends and her promise fulfilled.

I'll send help.

No one was coming for them. The FBI didn't know where her friends had gone. Her captors had moved them, and the possibilities were endless. Kacey knew that the Russians could vanish in plain sight. It was a game of days, days that her friends did not have.

Kacey lifted her sleepy baby and carried him inside on shaking legs. There, she tucked him into his bassinet and kissed him on the forehead. Then she turned to the job of collecting all she needed.

With all the toys and stuffed animals her tribe had left in the cabin, it was easy for Kacey to create a bundle that was the approximate size and shape of a newborn. One of the baby dolls seemed convincing when partially draped with a baby blanket, and an extra baby blanket filled out the doppelgänger's shape nicely. She left a hastily scrawled note under Charlie, whose full belly and fresh diaper ensured that he would sleep for a time. Kacey pressed her lips to the soft place on the top of his head as she prayed for his safety. Then she straightened and shook herself.

Colt had no means to rescue his comrades and he carried the burden of that truth each day. But she had a chance, a slim, dangerous chance, and she was as much a warrior as any here.

She had promised to send help. But she never expected the help would be her.

They wanted Charlie. So let them come and take him from her. If she failed, she would be satisfied that she had done all she could to save Marta, Brenda, Maggie and now Louisa. The knife in her boot ensured that, this time, she was not defenseless.

Kacey checked Colt's mobile phone and saw two

missed calls, both from Jake. She didn't play the message as she opened the door of the cabin, carrying the swaddled doll.

Her plan would depend on several things: that the FBI and tribal police were correct in their beliefs that the clinic was indeed involved in the disappearances and that the clinic would quickly inform her captors of her arrival. After that, either the Russians or the Wolf Posse needed to attempt to capture Charlie and not kill her. Finally, she needed to contact help and lead them to her friends.

Even if the Russians didn't take her or did not take her to the same place as her friends, the FBI would at least have her captors.

Kacey thought about the possibility of having to surrender her life to save her friends. She did not wish to die, but she did not wish to go on knowing that she hadn't done all she could to find them. It would kill her bit by bit, wondering and waiting for the lost that never came back.

She hoped Colt could forgive her.

Kacey cast one look back at Charlie and choked on the lump that rose in her throat. Would she ever see him again? The ache grew, spreading outward from her heart. Colt would protect him. She was certain. She had to be.

She stepped out on the porch and waved to the

sentry. He nodded and turned back to watching the road. After all, any abduction threat would come from outside their lines. She walked beside Lori's car, seeing Lori's purse, tote and nylon lunch bag on the passenger seat. Kacey opened the door and popped the latch for the trunk. Then she eased the door closed. A glance about showed that the sentry on the road still stared off toward the entrance and the one before the lodge watched the river.

It took only an instant for Kacey to roll into the trunk and close the door.

COLT RODE THE chopper Ty had loaned him. The Harley had been waiting before one of the cabins, delivered by Ty or Jake, Colt did not know. Somehow driving the motorcycle did not make him feel trapped. Rather he felt free. He made it to Ty's place, arriving in his driveway around eleven in the morning. Ty knew things that went on here on the rez, things the tribal leadership and tribal members never knew. Mostly, Ty kept this information to himself. Colt hoped Ty might make an exception for his kid brother.

Since his discharge from the US Marines, Ty fixed cars, detailed cars, rebuilt cars and, occasionally, sold cars. But he preferred working on the beautiful, old classics.

Colt spotted his truck parked before the open bay door. He parked and left the bike, finding Ty in the garage, beyond the bay door with his head under the hood of a Pontiac GTO with a dented side door. The tires were flat and the trunk showed more rust than blue paint.

"That's a beauty," he said.

Ty straightened but did not turn. There was a tension in his shoulders. Was he surprised to hear Colt's voice?

After all, though Ty had been to his place many times since his return to Turquoise Canyon, Colt rarely let Ty see him and they had spoken only when Colt asked to borrow Ty's bike.

Finally, Ty glanced over his shoulder at Colt, dark eyes narrowing against the bright morning light. After a moment, the crooked mischievous smile appeared. If he guessed at Colt's mission, his open expression gave no clue.

"Original matching numbers and only 39,000 miles," said Ty.

"She's fine. 1970?" Colt guessed.

"1967."

Ty's hair was cut at his jawline and was perpetually dropping before his eyes, yet he never drew it back. His smile always seemed more challenge than mirth, and his bright dark eyes swept over his baby brother. Colt was certain he didn't miss a single detail.

He didn't ask why Colt was here or exclaim on his decision to travel and speak.

"I got her at auction," he said, motioning to his current work in progress. "When I'm finished with her, I should make out pretty good unless I keep her. I'm tempted." Ty wiped his hands on a greasy rag and leaned back on the grille, waiting. Ty had a way of looking completely at ease in any situation.

Colt's second oldest brother had given him his first ride, a 1957 Chevy, mint green with pinstripes and an elaborate airbrush painting of a running mustang—a colt—on the front fender. It was waiting for him on his discharge. Now it sat before Ty's garage.

Colt thumbed at the truck. "You brought it here?"

"Jake did. He also brought my bike to the compound. See, you found it. Would have told you but, you know. You don't answer your phone."

Colt pressed a hand to his empty front pocket. He'd forgotten his phone.

"You just missed Abbie," said Ty.

Colt felt an instant stab of guilt. He hadn't even seen their kid sister since his return to the rez. "Yeah?"

"She pedals over here on her bike sometimes."

"How is she?" Colt asked.

"Tall. Nearly as tall as me."

Abbie was fourteen and growing by the minute. "She asks about you."

Colt said nothing to this.

"You should go see them."

Colt nodded. He should. But he wouldn't. Not yet.

Ty lifted a wrench and motioned in the direction Colt had come from. "Kinda far from the tribal gathering grounds, aren't you?"

"Kacey wants me to ask you to ask them to call it off."

Ty looked down at the spotless wrench, polishing it with the rag. "Can't."

"You did it for Jake and Lori."

"Different situation. The Russians had a backup."

"Backup?"

"Another girl with the same baby. Same parents, I mean. Boy, I think."

Colt felt sick. His mouth twisted in disgust. How could Ty be mixed up in this? "What do they do with the backups if…?"

Ty pressed his mouth tight and shook his head. "Don't know. Don't want to know. Didn't know anything until Jake dragged me back in. Faras did me a favor and reported to the Russians that Zella miscarried. So no baby girl to look for."

Colt's eyes rounded. What had Ty done for Faras in return? "You pay back the debt?"

"Not yet." Ty's brow lifted. Was he surprised that Colt understood exactly what Jake's favor had cost?

Then another possibility crept into his consciousness like a slug on a piece of ripe fruit.

Was that favor Kacey? Kacey and Charlie? Colt looked back the way he had come, wishing he had never left her. The hitch in his breathing and the pain in his heart told him what he should have seen before. He wasn't protecting Kacey because she asked him. He was protecting her because he still loved her. Now that love might bring him to have to fight his brother Ty.

Colt knew that, because of the favor he had done for Jake, Ty couldn't refuse Faras Pike. If Faras demanded Ty turn over his kid brother, his brother's girl and the baby, then Ty would do it or suffer the consequences.

He looked back at Ty and saw the resignation there. Ty recognized that Colt had worked it out.

"You know where they are keeping her friends?"

Ty set the wrench aside on the pink cloth draped over the open hood but maintained control of the greasy rag. He didn't answer.

"Do you?"

Ty twisted the rag. "Colt, listen—"

"Can you find out?"

"Not without joining the gang again. Faras would like that. Cut me out as a middleman."

Colt did not know exactly what Ty did for the Wolf Posse besides the obvious, supplying them with fast cars, cars that were much faster than, say, a state trooper's cruiser.

He wished Ty had never joined the Wolf Posse in the first place. Their home life had been hell when he joined, or that was what Jake had told him. They had all been afraid of their father, with good reason. But he'd only ever hit Ty.

"Is it Kacey?" asked Colt.

Ty didn't patronize him by pretending not to understand the question. "He hasn't asked. Yet. But I heard where she is, so they know." He draped the rag over the shoulder of his T-shirt. "You heading home, Colt?"

"To the compound?"

Ty shook his head. "To your cabin."

This was a warning and advice, all in one. Ty didn't want him to go back to Kacey and Charlie. He didn't want to have to do anything that would hurt his brother. Colt felt the same way, but some situations could not be avoided.

"I'm going back to her. She's determined to find her friends."

"Only way she sees them again is if they catch

her." Ty's stare was cold as ice water. "And then *you* won't find her."

Colt's heart frosted over. That was what Kacey had been planning. "FBI offered her relocation."

Ty nodded. "She should take it."

"I'm in love with her."

Ty's hard expression dropped and Colt saw the sorrow. The tough big brother who was always there for him now had eyes filling with tears.

"Then you should go, too. Soon."

Colt hugged Ty, and Ty squeezed him so tight it took his breath. When had he grown to the same height as his big brother?

Ty broke away first.

Colt wiped his eyes. "Jake is looking at you."

Ty blew out a breath. "Figures. No good deed… Maybe I can get a cell near Pop."

It had only been because of Kenshaw Little Falcon that Ty had been allowed to join the Marines instead of facing prosecution like their father after the armed robbery.

Colt studied the dust clinging to his boots.

The cell phone in Ty's back pocket vibrated. He drew it out and stared at the screen. "It's the favorite son." He turned the phone so Colt could see Jake's name. Then he answered the call.

Colt could hear Jake's voice because it was loud and held a note of alarm.

"Have you seen Colt?"

"Why?"

"Because Kacey is missing. Have you seen them?"

Colt's body stiffened as the downpour of panic washed over him.

OLEG PICKED UP the phone and grunted into the receiver. Their contact at the clinic was now refusing to provide new girls, the chickenshit.

"She's here," said his contact. "Kacey Doka. She just walked into Urgent Care."

"It's a trap," said Oleg.

"I think so, too. But you said to call if—"

"She alone?"

"Yes."

"Trap," Oleg repeated. Why else would she show up alone at the clinic?

"She has the baby."

Oleg thought it stank. And that was why he would pass it off on the bangers on the rez. Let them eat their own, and if they did manage to snatch the girl, so much the better. "I'll send someone."

"I don't know how long she'll be here—"

Oleg hung up. Then he called Faras Pike.

KACEY DID NOT know whom she had expected but certainly not Colt's older brother Ty. But there he was, striding toward her.

By way of a greeting, he said, "Jake called Colt and told us you were missing. He sent me and he's pissed."

Kacey frowned. She tried to act as if she believed him, but she could not control the trembling. Neither tribal police nor the FBI had yet arrived. So, what Ty said might be true, but it was just as likely that the Wolf Posse had sent Ty Redhorse for her.

She held the bundle of blankets and baby doll close as she walked with Ty out of the urgent-care center. Why, of all the possibilities, did it have to be him? Colt's big brother, the one he looked up to and loved. Maybe he'd never have to know.

Ty led the way and she followed him, climbing into his muscle car, some kind of Pontiac from the seventies that looked as if it had just come off the line instead of out of a field somewhere.

"Is that purple?"

"Violet metallic with black interior. Seventy-three Plymouth Hemi Barracuda."

"It's…" *Garish*, she thought.

"Fast," he said, finishing her sentence.

He held open the door for her. She spotted a huge, familiar dog sitting on a blanket on the back seat.

She offered her hand, and Hemi licked her. "Good to see you, girl," she said.

Kacey slipped inside and Ty closed the door. She glanced around as the tingle of fear lifted the hairs on her arms.

Ty slid behind the wheel and set them in motion.

She wondered how long she had to pretend she didn't suspect that he was not taking her to Colt.

He blew out a blast of air. His expression was no longer calm. Instead his jaw clamped and his brow arched as he cast her an angry stare.

"What did you drag me into, Kacey?" asked Ty.

And then she knew. It was Ty, the one they had sent. Not Oleg or Anton or the one whose name she did not even know. Not a banger in a yellow Mustang wearing gang colors. They sent someone she trusted to take her.

She sat back and stared out at the road ahead. "Where are you taking me?"

"Damned if I know."

Chapter Fourteen

Kacey eyed Ty with a mixture of disappointment and dread. "I should have guessed."

"You should have. And you should have listened to Colt and stayed put. What'd you think, you could bust this thing up all by your lonesome?"

She had only thought that her sacrifice might provide a lead. It hadn't.

"He doesn't think you're in the Wolf Posse, you know," she said.

"Best he never finds out."

"I saw this in a movie once. They sent the man's best friend to kill him."

"This isn't a movie. And I'm not here to kill you, but you're killing me."

"Does this repay the favor you owe Faras Pike?"

"How do you know about that?"

"Officer Redhorse has a baby that the Russians want or would want if they knew about her. Surely

Pike knows. You're the only one I can think of who could make him go deaf and blind."

"You got it all worked out, huh?"

She gave him a satisfied smile.

"You call the FBI?" he asked.

"No," she said.

He cast her a long look. "You wearing a wire, Kacey?"

She shook her head. "Where would I get one of those?"

"At the compound before you stowed away in Lori Redhorse's car."

"You think the FBI would let me do this?"

"Well, you must have some plan. Either that or you have a death wish. So now might be a good time to fill me in."

"Why should I tell you anything?"

"Because I'm the guy Colt sent for you."

A bubble of hope rose inside her.

"Lucky, because I'm also the guy who talked Faras into sending me instead of your mother."

"My…my mother? What are you saying?" She swiveled in her seat to face him, holding the bundle to her body as if it were a real baby.

"Kacey, she's a mule. Been working for the Posse for years. You have to have known that."

Kacey knew what a mule was. It was someone

who carried drugs from one place to another. She knew her mother used drugs and that she disappeared for long stretches, but she had never put together the pieces that had been given to her until Ty threw them in her lap all tied up with a bow.

She couldn't stop shaking her head in disbelief, even though she believed him. "I didn't know."

Ty snorted. "Then you didn't want to know."

The knot in her stomach spread to her chest, constricting her breathing. What did he mean, her mother? "They wouldn't send my mother."

Ty's reply was a snort of disgust.

"How can I believe anything you say?"

"I don't know. Most folks don't."

But Colt trusted him and Kacey trusted Colt.

Ty headed back through Koun'nde toward Piñon Forks.

"My opinion," he said, "you should have turned your mother over to tribal police years ago. What I would have done."

Kacey thought of his father, Colton, now serving time in federal prison for a job in which he had enlisted Ty as his getaway driver. If anyone knew about terrible parenting, it was Ty.

"Lucky for you, you didn't have to. Tribal arrested him for you," she said. She readjusted the mannequin and checked it as if it were really Charlie.

"Who were you talking to on the phone outside the clinic?"

So she'd been spotted before she'd even entered the FEMA trailer. She'd called Jake Redhorse, asked him to phone Agent Forrest and given him her location.

"Who is it?" she asked.

"Who is who?" asked Ty.

"At the clinic. Is it Kee?"

"All I know is what I'm told. So here I am like a good little lapdog." He glowered at her. "Chances are high they will kill you and take him."

"And you?"

"Survivor, same as always."

"Where are we going?"

"To the Russians."

"Darabee? Is Colt there?"

"I sure hope so," said Ty. "He should be, unless they caught him already. Tribal police are behind us somewhere. I called Jake. First time we've had a conversation lasting more than a minute in years. Please tell me that the FBI can track you."

"They should. I have Colt's mobile phone."

"Where is it?"

She hesitated.

He eyed the baby doll. "Inside the blankets?" he guessed.

She lifted the swaddled doll protectively and said nothing.

Ty motioned a thumb toward the bundle. "That's not Charlie."

"How do you know that?" she asked.

"Hasn't moved." He thumbed to the rear seat and his sleeping dog. "And Hemi showed no interest. She'd definitely notice a baby in the car and give it a thorough sniffing. So that doesn't smell like a baby. Plus, you would never bring a baby where you are going."

She laid the toy across her lap, surrendering the ruse.

"When they figure that out, you are out of time."

She tried not to let the panic block her throat, but her words held a certain strain. "I promised them I'd bring help."

He gave a slow shake of his head as if she was not to be believed. "Getting yourself killed won't help."

"Neither will hiding," she said.

He pressed his mouth into a hard line and said nothing.

"What do you know about the exchange?" she asked.

"Where, when and who. Ten minutes, Antelope Lake Overlook and you are expected by two Russians." He made the turn away from the river road, away from Piñon Forks. This way led past Turquoise Lake to Red Rock Dam to the west. Beyond that was a steep winding road along the cliff face that led down the mountain to Antelope Lake. Between the dam and the lake was a spectacular overlook that included a picnic table and a trail down to the bottom of the dam.

"Do you know where they're keeping my friends?" she asked.

Ty snorted. "I don't know anything except what Colt told me and what Faras told me. If I hang around after the drop, the FBI will arrest me. If I don't hang around, Colt might get himself killed. If you don't survive, Colt will blame me. If you do survive this ridiculousness, you can turn me in and I still go to jail. In other words, I'm having a really, really bad day."

Kacey held the hand grip as they entered the last switchback before the overlook. Signs warned of falling rock, and the shoulder of the road was punctuated with great hunks of stone that had rolled onto the road.

In the rear seat, Hemi rose to sit, trying vainly to maintain her balance as they hugged the final curve, making her rock into the car door. Ty liked fast cars and he knew how to drive them.

"Do you think they'll bring me to my friends?"

He gave her a pitying look. "They want the baby.

Not you. You are a liability because you've seen them and you can be replaced, have been already if what Colt said is true. Louisa Tah," he said, mentioning the newest missing girl. "Right? And if they don't get that baby you carried, they'll just feed the waiting parents some story about the fetus not being viable and call a do-over."

"But if we can capture one of the men who held me…?"

"Then what? They'll give up and lead you to your friends?" He gave a strangled sound that fell between laughter and a growl. "They'll die first. Kacey, you're young and inexperienced, so I'll give you a pass on this. But your plan sucks." He eased on the brakes. "We're here. Now take out that phone and dial Luke Forrest's number. Then mute the call and put it on speaker."

She did as she was told and finished as they rolled into the dirt lot. The parking area was empty except for an eighteen-foot RV before which sat two lawn chairs beneath an awning. Between the seats sat a large forest green cooler with cup holders molded into the lid.

"They aren't here yet," she said.

Ty glanced at the ceiling and blew out a breath. Then he cast her a sidelong glance. "Look again."

She scanned the empty stretch of sand and then

came back to the RV. It looked so completely normal…
just like the house in which she had been held. Kacey
shivered.

"Exactly."

"Where's Colt?" She had a sinking feeling Ty had
only dangled that hope before her to keep her from
doing something stupid. Or perhaps more stupid.

Ty leaned forward, his chest nearly pressed to
the wheel as he glanced around. "Don't know. High
ground, I hope. He's a hell of a good shot. But so are
they." He thumbed toward the RV.

He smoothly turned the muscle car in a half circle so that her door faced the trailer at a distance of
about twenty feet.

"Get out," he ordered. "If you hear shots, get down
and stay down. And do *not* get in that trailer."

Kacey hesitated.

"Out," he said.

She lifted the doll to her chest, feeling the squar-
ish lump of Colt's cell phone tucked inside the baby
blanket. Then she opened the door. She had barely
gained her feet when Ty peeled out, his passenger door slamming shut as he performed a perfect
doughnut, raising a cloud of dust.

Anton stepped from inside the camper first, holding a black semiautomatic weapon at his hip. He
motioned to her with his opposite hand and she re-

mained where she was, coughing and fanning at the stinging dust. Behind Anton, Oleg appeared in the open door.

Ty continued to perform his show of motor muscle, making one more circle before fishtailing out of the parking area. His tires sent another wave of dust back at them.

Anton glanced around the empty overlook parking area and came toward her, his outline obscured by the fine swirling cloud of red dust.

"Nowhere to run, Kacey," said Anton.

Kacey remembered Ty's warning. If she got in that RV, she was dead. She turned tail and ran toward the worst of the swirling dust, following the course Ty had taken and running as fast as her legs would carry her.

COLT WATCHED HIS brother Ty turn his '73 'Cuda in circles in the dirt, covering his previously spotless hood with grime and giving Kacey the cover she needed to run away from her pursuers. From his vantage point, the Russians should have made easy targets, but the dust also prevented him from getting a bead on them.

But he heard them. They were shouting at Kacey as she ran. He hadn't counted on the nerve-jolting fear that seeing Kacey in jeopardy would bring. His mouth was as dry as the dirt beneath him and he couldn't muster the spit to swallow.

Colt feared they would reach her before he could take them both down. That forced him to leave cover and charge out in the open toward her.

He made his move, streaking across the lot with the rifle raised. He debated calling to her because she was running at an angle that would take her away from him but closer to the cover of the rocks positioned to prevent inattentive sightseeing drivers from plunging into the canyon.

But if he called to her, he would reveal his presence before he had a shot off and possibly bring her between him and his targets. He could see them more clearly now and noticed that one held a semiautomatic weapon pointing at Kacey. The shoulder strap across the chest of the other man meant he might also have a similar weapon.

Kacey spotted him now and her stride faltered. She turned toward him and managed three more steps before her pursuer caught her, stretching out a hand and capturing her arm at the same time he noticed Colt.

The Russian bellowed and swung his semiautomatic toward Colt as Colt squeezed off a round, sending a bullet into the Russian's chest. Bullets sprayed the ground before Colt, forcing him to dive clear and then roll to his feet. Kacey dropped to a crouch, protecting the bundle he knew was not Charlie. Her pursuer grasped her loose hair and tugged Kacey up before him. He released his weapon, which swung on its strap to his side, and used his free hand to cover the bullet wound on his right side. Then he used Kacey as a shield as he retreated. His partner fired at Colt.

Colt scrambled for cover, reaching one of the large boulders that edged the lot. When he peeked from cover, it was to see Kacey's captor still dragging her backward toward the RV. The second man kept Colt pinned in position with a barrage of lead as the first pulled Kacey toward the steps.

There was a struggle as she dropped the baby doll and slashed at the arm of her captor with a boot knife. His boot knife, he realized.

Her captor howled in pain as he released her. Kacey dropped to the ground and rolled beneath the camper, knocking over one of the lawn chairs. The second man retrieved the bundle, lifted it and then gave a roar of rage as he threw the dummy over the precipice. Then he sank to his knees and sent a spray of bullets after Kacey.

Something inside Colt snapped. He stood, aimed and squeezed off three well-placed rounds, dropping both men. He was sure he hit each in the upper thorax, but they were both still able to crawl after Kacey and away from him.

"Should have taken head shots," he muttered and followed his moving targets. Were they wearing body armor? His cartridge rounds still should have defeated Kevlar.

Kacey appeared at the back of the trailer at the same moment that two dusty black sedans skidded into the entrance of the overlook lot. The FBI had finally arrived.

The second gunman charged the cars with his semiautomatic, spraying bullets across the reinforced glass of the windshield. The first vehicle did not slow as it hit the gunman, carrying him along on the fender before pinning him to the side of the RV where he slumped across the hood.

Colt saw Kacey scramble down the embankment followed by her remaining pursuer. The man let his weapon dangle from the arm strap over his shoulder as he hurried after Kacey. He gripped his right hand over his forearm and the wound Kacey had given him as blood seeped through his fingers. The right side of his back was crimson with blood from Colt's first shot. Lung shot, Colt decided, but even with only one lung, the Russian continued after Kacey.

Colt knew the signs. The man was trapped, shot and desperate. But he had not given up on his objective and he still had enough time and enough blood in him to kill Kacey. Colt took aim. No mistakes this time.

He aimed for the man's head and squeezed the trigger just as the man dropped to his seat and slid down the embankment after Kacey. Colt's bullet sped out into the empty space where his target's head had been.

KACEY GLANCED BACK at the sound of metal striking metal. Part of the RV now jutted past the embankment. What had hit it? She prayed it was the FBI. A second glance showed her that Anton was sliding down the trail behind her on his backside. He released his bloody arm to grip his weapon, giving Kacey just enough time to scramble off the trail.

Unfortunately this switchback was a steep grade that offered nothing but cactus and loose rock to stop her as she clawed at the sliding rock that fell along with her. She landed hard on her back on the flat spot that was the trail. Kacey stared up at the blue cloudless sky as her lungs refused to obey her command to breathe. Colt's knife lay in her open palm, and her other arm dangled over the precipice that marked the next switchback in the trail.

She caught movement and saw Anton on the trail above, taking aim at her. The air rushed back into her lungs, dry and hot. Anton lifted his weapon in a bloody hand and Kacey closed her fist on the knife. She would not risk another slide down the cliff face. She knew the trail well enough to remember that this next section included stairs and a sheer drop. So she would have to face Anton or die trying. She sat up, drawing her arm back and throwing the knife as Colt had taught her.

COLT PURSUED THE Russian chasing Kacey. Colt was fast and agile from years spent climbing up and down such cliffs and he closed the distance. The Russian moved slowly, gripping the rock some ten feet below Colt. Below him, his target directed his weapon at Kacey.

She threw her knife. Her pursuer ducked as the blade spun and then flashed past his head, striking the cliff face beside him, falling to the trail at his feet. Then he straightened and aimed his weapon at Kacey. Colt knew that this time he would kill her.

"Hey!" yelled Colt at the same time he targeted the man in his sights. Kacey's pursuer glanced back in time to hear the click that signaled Colt's rifle jamming. Colt tried again with the same result.

The Russian turned back to face Kacey.

Colt released his rifle so it swung on its shoulder strap and then he dived off the trail toward the Russian. The weight of his body took them both over the lip of the trail and out into space.

The Russian screamed. Colt had a perfect view of the trail below the switchback, just a little too far away for them to land safely. Beyond was nothing but the air between him and the lake that lay far, far below. In that moment, he saw each rock and the gaping shock on Kacey's face as he and her attacker sailed past.

Chapter Fifteen

Kacey scrambled to her feet when Colt tackled Anton from the switchback above her. She had only a moment, a lifetime, to judge the distance and recognized that neither of the men locked together would land on the path. Colt was leaving her behind again. Her reaction was swift. She dived as well with only the single thought to stop him. Catch him. Hold him. Keep him.

She could not keep him from joining the US Marines. She could not keep him from choosing to live like a hermit in the woods. She could not keep him with her when she left the reservation. But she could keep him from sailing over the cliff and out of her life forever.

Her hands clamped on his leg and she latched on with all her might. Some part of her brain screamed a shrieking siren of distress, like a tripped fire alarm, as her instincts fought against her will for survival. Her added weight only changed the direction of Colt's descent. But not enough. If she didn't let go, they'd carry her over, as well.

She didn't let go.

Instead, she drew her body forward and clung to his leg as Colt released Anton. The Russian was now as free as the wind, a flightless bird sailing out into the blue sky above the river.

She hit the rough rock and gravel beside the trail first. Kacey's stomach landed on Colt's leg and foot, driving the wind from her lungs again. Her shirt and jeans shredded beneath her. She saw stars as they slid along the rock and sand. Colt's hips and chest bounced on the ground and then slid over the edge. Kacey cried out, a strangled sound, and closed her eyes, bracing for the inevitable fall.

Some long-buried instinct caused her to spread her legs wide and hook her feet, making a sort of anchor. She felt the vibrations of the earth dragging beneath her toes all the way up to her jaw.

It took a moment to realize that they were no longer moving. Kacey blinked open her eyes. Her fingers locked tighter around the loose fabric of Colt's jeans. Her cheek was resting in the crook behind his knee. Her elbows and legs stung as if she had scraped away all the skin there.

She could see Colt's hind end but not his upper body.

"Colt," she shouted.

"Don't let go, Kacey."

Oh, she wouldn't. She wasn't letting him go ever again because she loved him. It was the only explanation for her actions. She let the truth settle over her with the dust. It didn't solve anything. He still wanted to remain on the rez and she still wanted to leave it behind, take her baby and go somewhere safe where girls were not taken like spring lambs. But her love had saved his life, just as he had saved hers.

She felt him twisting. One of his arms appeared, reaching back, clawing at the ground. Gradually, he hauled his chest back onto the trail. Only when he was entirely on solid ground did she ease up on her hold. Colt rolled to his back and she crawled on her bleeding hands and knees to reach him.

"I got you," she said.

He wrapped an arm around her. "He can't hurt you again," he said and let his head drop back to the solid ground beneath them.

For the next few moments, she just breathed in the familiar earthy scent of him, her eyes closed at the sweetness of their survival. The difference between life and death, at times, came into sharp contrast.

"That was dangerous," he said.

She chuckled. Everything hurt, which meant she was alive. "Not as dangerous as diving headfirst off a cliff."

Now he chuckled. His arm around her tightened. "True."

"Is he...?"

Colt laid his free hand across his eyes, his breathing labored. "Not sure." His body shuddered. "I thought he'd kill you."

She lifted her arm to examine her elbow. Blood oozed from several gravel-filled wounds. He sat up and cradled one of her hands, turning it gently.

"We have to clean these up."

Kacey looked toward the cliff a mere three inches from Colt's hip. In her mind, she saw him sailing over her and thought of what might have been. Kacey's throat burned and her vision went blurry as the tears came in great choking sobs.

He gathered her up in his arms and she clung to him, reveling in the warm, solid comfort of his body. He was still here with her and she thanked God for it.

Kacey pushed past the fear, finding her voice.

"I—I almost l-lost you," she said between sobs.

Colt stroked her head and dropped kisses there as

he murmured assurances. She was safe. Charlie was safe. He'd bring her home to him.

She wanted to tell him that she had been afraid for him. Afraid of losing him. But then another fear rose in her heart. What if, now that she was safe, he would let her go?

"You found them. The men who took you," he said. "Maybe now the FBI will find your friends."

She nodded. Unable to speak past the aching lump in her throat.

"If I could have," he said, "I would have done the same for my friends."

She closed her eyes and a tear squeezed between her lids, trailing down her dusty cheek. He understood.

A moan came from the trail below them.

Colt looked over the edge. Kacey moved to her stomach, sprawling in order to safely peer down. The trail ran forty feet below them at an incline that consisted of a series of steps followed by open stretches.

Anton lay on one of the series of steps. There was blood trickling from his nose and mouth. His shirt was soaked with blood from the bullet wound. He stared up at them and spoke in Russian. His eyes had a vacant expression and his mouth gaped open when he finished.

"Anton?" called Kacey.

"Can't move my legs," he said.

Colt spoke to her. "Look at his body. The angle. I think he broke his back."

She replied in a tone just above a whisper. "Look at the blood."

"I don't know how he survived."

Anton lifted a hand. "Give me a gun."

Colt snorted. "Yeah, right," he said.

"A knife, then."

"He wants to kill himself," said Kacey to Colt, certain she was right.

"And rob the FBI of a witness," said Colt. "No way. He knows where your friends are or he knows who knows. He's not checking out."

Kacey agreed. They needed him to find Marta and the others. He was their best chance at that.

"Please," said Anton.

"You live," said Colt, his words a decree.

Anton moaned, his blood bubbling up from his mouth.

"He won't live long if we don't get help," she said.

Colt pressed to his feet and offered her his hand. "Can you walk?"

In answer, she took his hand and allowed him to draw her up beside him.

A familiar voice came from above them. "You two all right?"

They turned simultaneously and saw Lieutenant Luke Forrest standing above them on the trail.

"About time," said Colt.

"Had trouble with your position. Signal kept going in and out."

"Mountains," said Colt.

"Where's the other one?" asked Forrest.

Colt thumbed over his shoulder. Forrest lifted his radio.

"He run?"

Kacey shook her head. "Fell."

"Can't move or so he says," added Colt. "Bleeding to death."

A moment later, four FBI agents in navy blazers jogged down the trail, paused briefly at Forrest for instructions and then hurried past Colt and Kacey, disappearing around the turn. Kacey watched them reappear below them.

"Let's get you two out of here."

Kacey let Colt guide her up the trail. Normally steady when facing climbing or heights, she found her legs unstable and her body jolting and shivering as if determined to ignore all her instructions.

"Kacey?" Colt said. "You are really pale."

Her knees gave way then. He caught her in his arms and lifted her.

"I don't know what's wrong with me."

"Shock," he said. Then he called to Forrest, "Ambulance en route?"

"Yes. Fire and rescue."

Colt met Forrest on the hairpin, but Colt wouldn't let him take Kacey and he made the rest of the upward climb in record time.

"The other one?" asked Kacey. "Oleg?"

"Pinned against the RV. Shot himself in the head. He's dead."

Her heart sank as the chances of finding her friends flickered. Was it all for nothing?

The sound of sirens reached them, coming from below them, down the mountain.

Kacey remembered reaching the overlook, still safe in Colt's arms. She caught a glimpse of Oleg's body sprawled over the hood of the truck that pinned him in place to the RV. Something was wrong with the top of his head. Kacey realized what she was seeing, the aftereffects of a bullet through his skull, and looked away too late.

Colt muttered, "He got off easy."

He set her in the shade, in the lawn chair beneath the canopy. She watched with a frightening disinterest while the rescue trucks rolled in. They had to shout at her to make her understand. Cleaning her wounds brought her back, the sting and the abrasions of the gravel embedded in the long scrapes that ran down her thighs and over her elbows. She looked at the bright blood and wondered how she had ever held on to Colt. Because she had to, she decided. And now they were safe and she would be a protected witness and Colt would go back home to Turquoise Canyon.

They carried Anton past her on a spine board. He turned to fix her with a steady stare, cursing at her in the language that she had begun to understand over her months of captivity.

"Did he say where they are?" she asked the EMT before her.

"Where who are, honey?" she asked.

Where was Colt? She had not noticed him leaving her. She wanted to say goodbye and tell him that she loved him. It wouldn't be enough to get him to come with her. She knew that. But she also knew that she could not stay on Turquoise Canyon Reservation. The men and women of Tribal Thunder had important work, and her presence there was keeping them from protecting others. It was time to go.

They took her to the hospital in Darabee. She rode in the ambulance with one of the FBI agents. He said Colt had to stay at the overlook.

Kacey's breasts ached, her body ached and she missed Charlie. She asked for him. But all they gave her was intravenous fluids.

"Will they find my friends?" asked Kacey.

"We are looking. That RV will help us, and apprehending one of the two suspects will help us. You did well, Ms. Doka. But now you need to rest and let us do our jobs."

"They kept me for eight months," she told the agent.

He nodded. The EMT checked her blood pressure, so she had to stretch her neck to see the agent. "I think being paralyzed will be worse."

The agent nodded again.

At the hospital, they checked her through the ER and later moved her upstairs, rolling her to the elevator and down one corridor after another. She managed the transfer from gurney to bed with only a little help. Her room smelled of floor wax and chicken broth. She had a view of the clear blue sky and an AC unit that whistled like the wind down the canyons.

She was so tired. But she kept asking for Charlie. Finally, Agent Luke Forrest arrived and told her that Lori Redhorse had Charlie and said that he would remain on Turquoise Canyon rez until Kacey could come and get him herself.

Kacey smiled. Charlie was safe. Jake and Lori Redhorse would protect her baby until she could get back to him.

Agent Forrest drew a chair up beside her bed.

"It was a dangerous thing you did," said Forrest. "Foolish."

"I wanted to find my friends. I promised."

"You might have died out there."

"I didn't find them," said Kacey. "You didn't. Did you?"

The slow shake of his head crushed the tiny flutter of hope.

"We are getting closer," said Forrest.

"It was for nothing?"

"No. We now know which mob is involved. This organization is, well, extensive. So we're expanding our search, checking other Native tribes and their lists of runaways. We're afraid there may be more of you."

Kacey swallowed. "How many more?"

"We don't know. There are a lot of missing women. But thanks to you, they are starting a special task force."

Kacey turned away. *A task force.* She felt like crying again.

"It's important, Kacey. What you did."

"I failed. I didn't find them." And she knew now that she might never find them. They might be among the forever lost. And she would have to learn to live with that, just like Colt was trying to do.

Everyone in her tribe knew someone, a sister, a

daughter or a friend, who had disappeared. It was all too common and not just in her tribe. All over the country. Native American women went missing and were never found. She was lucky. Marta was not. Kacey closed her eyes and said farewell to the friends that she could not rescue. And cursed herself for the promise she could not keep. "I promised I would send help."

"Kacey, there was a GPS in the RV," said Forrest. "We reversed the directions and backtracked. We found a camp out in the desert near San Carlos Reservation. There were girls there. Twenty-three, all like you and your friends. We found them because of you, Kacey. You did send help. Those captives are free because of you."

Tears spilled from her eyes and rolled down her temples to soak into her hair. It had not been for nothing. They had found some of them. Kacey covered her eyes with her hands and wept. As the sobs continued, she crooked her arm over her eyes.

Agent Forrest rubbed her shoulder, and when she lowered her bandaged arm from across her eyes, he sat back.

"We'll keep looking for your friends, Kacey. We won't stop. But you need to stop now."

She met his gaze and saw the determination there.

He wouldn't give up and there was nothing more she could do in the hunt.

"Yes," she said.

"I have talked to the Justice Department about you, Kacey. We believe that Anton's survival will ensure that someone else will be coming after you and Charlie."

She wasn't safe here. Her gaze darted to the door and then back to Forrest.

"We would like to relocate you."

She nearly forgot to breathe. She wanted that, too. But she still had ties to the rez.

"What about my sisters and brothers?" She was afraid to leave them with her mom and she was afraid to tell Forrest what Ty had revealed about her mother's work with the gang. As much as Kacey longed to get away, she would not do so at the expense of her siblings.

Forrest looked away. "They have already been placed within your tribe."

She'd been removed to foster care a time or two. They always sent them back to their mom.

"For how long?"

"It's permanent this time. Your mother has given up custody."

Kacey's brow sank. "She would never do that."

"Kacey, I have really hard news. Your mother was involved in your disappearance."

Her words were a whisper. "That's not true."

"She's admitted to accepting payment for you, Kacey."

Kacey's ears began to buzz and she thought she might be sick. She clamped a hand over her mouth, breathing through her nose.

"She's addicted to heroin," said Forrest. "We got a tip, so we've been watching her since your return. She's been moving drugs. We caught her and she's facing felony charges."

A tip? Was that Ty? No, he'd never rat out a member of the gang. But Ty had been right. Her mother had been a gang member all along.

And her mother was going to prison. Just like Colt's father. Kacey's hand dropped from her mouth as the shock was replaced with a dull numbness. She felt anesthetized and did not know if she should be happy or sad about the news regarding her mother. Both, she decided, all tied up in a hard knot in her stomach.

Agent Forrest kept on talking. "She made a deal with the DA. Reduced sentence in exchange for all she knows about this case. She helped the Wolf Posse pick girls, Kacey. That's why your friends were taken. You and Marta were classmates. And Brenda was a teammate on your high-school volleyball team. Right?"

She had one hand pressed tight to her forehead

at this new shock but managed to nod. Her mother knew Brenda and Marta. Of course she did. The contents of Kacey's stomach heaved, threatening to come up. She swallowed hard. She squeezed her eyes shut to concentrate on breathing as saliva filled her mouth.

"I'm going to be sick," she promised.

Forrest had a pail before her in time. Afterward, he offered a damp washcloth. He would have made a good father, she thought, but Colt said that he was unmarried.

"You okay?" he asked.

"No."

He nodded his understanding.

"Your sisters are going with Jake Redhorse's mom and her husband, Burt Rope. You lived there awhile in high school, right?"

Mrs. Redhorse had some health issues, but she was a good woman and a good mother. Several times, she had given Kacey the kind of home she had always dreamed about during her difficult teen years.

"My brothers?" she asked and set aside the cloth. The heaving in her belly ceased, replaced by a squeezing tension.

"One of your tribal leaders has asked to foster them."

"Who?"

"Her name is Hazel Trans."

Mrs. Trans had been Kacey's absolute favorite teacher. She had recently retired and Kacey thought her brothers would be lucky indeed to have Mrs. Trans as a foster mother.

She nodded her approval and offered a smile. "Thank you."

"Sure," said Forrest. "Tomorrow you'll be discharged and we'll bring you back up to Turquoise Canyon to collect Charlie. If you like, we can arrange for you to see your siblings, too."

He didn't say *for the last time*, but that was the case. She was going and would not be coming back.

"In Darabee, someone tried to take Charlie," she said. "They changed the orders about feeding."

"We're looking into that. Creating a list of everyone who had access to those orders. We'll find whoever did that, Kacey. But it was not the FBI. We have no intention of separating you from Charlie."

Forrest gave her a warm smile and rose to go. He made it to the end of her bed and then snapped his fingers as if just remembering something. "I almost forgot. One loose end. Who drove you from the clinic to the meeting at the overlook, Kacey?"

It was Ty. She glanced away.

"Colt came on a motorcycle," said Forrest. "We

found the tracks and the bike, which belongs to his brother Ty. But how did you get there?"

"I—I don't remember." She met his gaze and saw the smile beneath the sharp hawkish eyes. He didn't believe her.

"Is that so? Any other gaps in your memory?"

"Just the clinic visits."

One dark brow arched over an eye. "I see."

Kacey forced herself to hold his gaze and not fidget. Her nose itched and her lips tingled. She did not like to lie, but she knew Ty was tied up in this somehow.

"Your deal with justice will depend on your complete honesty."

She held her silence. Ty had been ordered by the gang to transport her. But they had not ordered him to raise that dust or call Colt and be sure he knew where she was being taken. If she had to jeopardize her deal to protect him, she would.

Forrest looked away and then back. "Well, it should be easy to figure out. We have tire tracks and they're nearly nine-and-a-half inches wide. Classic muscle-car tire like for a Corvette or a Barracuda." He paused, watching her intently.

Her forehead felt damp with sweat.

"Nothing? Well, we'll find the car and then the driver. Have a few suspects."

It would probably be easier to find the car if the man who owned it did not also own a body shop. Kacey wondered if Ty's precious Barracuda was already in pieces.

She held the agent's gaze, determined not to implicate Ty, no matter what the consequence. Ty had helped them and she would not repay his kindness by turning him over to the FBI.

"My memory won't improve," she said. "If that jeopardizes my eligibility with the Justice Department, then so be it."

He rested a hand on his belt, his long fingers drumming on the black leather. "Did it occur to you that the Wolf Posse were the ones who delivered your friends over to the Russian mob? I wouldn't be protecting gang members, Kacey."

She said nothing.

"Care to tell me how you got to the meet?"

"I don't remember."

He snorted. "Well, we'll talk again soon. Maybe your recall will improve."

"Can I see Colt before I go with the Justice Department?"

"I don't see why not."

She wanted to ask why Colt had not come to see her here, in Darabee, but she did not because she was afraid of the answer. Would it be harder to leave without telling him her feelings or harder to admit that she loved him?

Chapter Sixteen

Colt finished with the FBI. He had done as Ty had asked and told them the truth. Ty had picked up Kacey because the Wolf Posse trusted him and knew that Kacey would come with him. He'd then called Colt and told him where they were heading. Colt had then called the FBI.

Ty was now safely back on tribal lands and Colt would do everything in his power to help keep him there until he had assurances that the FBI would not go after him for his part in recapturing Kacey. Until then, Ty would be a virtual prisoner on tribal land and would be lucky if the tribal leadership did not arrest him. The only good news regarding Ty was that Kenshaw Little Falcon had offered to represent Ty to the tribal council, which Colt found encouraging.

Colt contended that it was important that both the Russians and the Wolf Posse believed that Ty had done as he was ordered. If they didn't believe it, Ty would not keep breathing for long.

Forrest drove Colt back to Turquoise Canyon.

"No trouble driving in cars now?" he asked.

"Some," Colt admitted. "But I'm getting better." He did not admit that he continued to pretend that Charlie was in the car with him. Picturing Charlie here did two things at once. It grounded him in the reality that he was here on the rez and it also helped him believe that he was safe. Colt had talked about it with the therapist Kenshaw recommended, who assured him that such a simple trick was well worth using.

"We'll be bringing Kacey back to the rez tomorrow."

Just the sound of her name made his heartbeat increase.

"She wants to collect some of her things."

Colt's head snapped toward Forrest. "Collect?"

"She isn't staying, Colt. She wants to keep the child that she carried. We have no objections to that, but all evidence indicates that chances are high that both she and Charlie will continue to be targets if they stay."

She was going with the Justice Department. She had no other choice. She was leaving as she always wanted. And he was going back to his cabin in the woods.

Colt clamped down hard, locking his teeth together until the muscle at his jaw ached. Once all he had wanted was to get back to Turquoise Canyon and never leave again. Now he wanted Kacey and Charlie there with him.

His perfect picture of Kacey and Charlie coming home to him evaporated like the sweat on his forehead. He had to let them go, for her sake and for Charlie's.

KACEY RETURNED TO the compound along the river. Hazel Trans was there with her brothers. Her sisters arrived soon after with Burt Rope and Colt's mother and his kid sister, Abbie. The reunion was brief. She did not tell her brothers that this would be the last time she saw them. They were too young to understand.

It was a monumental relief that her sisters and brothers would be safe and well taken care of. She trusted Mrs. Trans and Colt's mother, May. Abbie was all smiles and laughter at the news that she would be gaining three new sisters. At fourteen, Abbie had given up hope that her mother would produce a sister. She asked Kacey where she would live. Colt told her they were still working that out.

Kacey took comfort in the certainty that May and Hazel would be there for her siblings. Kacey had called protective services on her mother the last time her mother left, and she'd caught hell for it. Now she wondered if that was what triggered her mother's decision to offer Kacey to the gang. Kacey was a threat to her, a growing threat.

Perhaps it was best that she would never know. She was not planning to see her mother before her trial or after.

"What if she wants them back?" she asked Mrs. Trans.

"I don't think she really does, Kacey. I've spoken to her. She isn't in a good place right now and she recognizes that."

Mrs. Trans hugged Kacey and then slid behind the wheel.

Hewitt spun in the rear seat, waving with enthusiasm as they drove away. It was her undoing. Shirley asked her what was wrong and she told them in a rush of tears and sobs that she had to go away.

Soon they were all crying and hugging. They asked her if it would ever be safe for them to return, and she had no answer. She knew only what the Justice Department had told her and what she now repeated to them. Her relocation was permanent and she would be safe only if she made no contact with the ones she left behind.

She knew she was lucky. She had escaped and would have a new life. She would attend college somewhere as she had always hoped and the Justice Department would arrange for all her needs. She expected to not require their support forever, but only until she was able to provide for herself and her son.

Her sisters left next. She hugged them each in turn, and the tears that ran down her cheeks mingled with theirs as they embraced for a final time.

"I'll never forget you," said Winnie.

Shirley would not even talk. When they were all in Burt Rope's car, Jackie broke away and ran back to her, giving her one more hug. And then they were gone.

Tomorrow she would see Colt for the last time and that was one parting that she did not think she could bear. She had lost her friends, her family, her home and her tribe. It seemed too much that she would lose Colt now after just finding him again.

But that was tomorrow's trouble, she thought. And then she heard the truck engine.

A familiar mint-green pickup truck rolled up to the lodge, and there behind the wheel was Colt Redhorse.

COLT FOUND KACEY standing still as one of the posts that supported the roof of the porch before the tribe's lodge. Only her eyes moved. In her arms, Charlie lay wrapped in a fuzzy baby blue blanket that trailed over Kacey's arm. She was wearing a button-up orange shirtdress tied at the waist. The short sleeves revealed the white gauze that circled both her forearms. The knee-length cotton hid the wounds on her knees and made her look older somehow. Perhaps that was because of her sad expression and the circles beneath her eyes.

Kacey was the oldest nineteen-year-old Colt knew. She was leaving them. But she was not leaving him. Not if he could help it.

He jumped down from the truck and reached her.

"They said you were coming tomorrow," she said.

"Couldn't wait." He reached for her, clasping her upper arm above the bandages and coming in for a brief kiss. Or he had meant it to be brief, but the contact was like a match dropped on dry paper, igniting into a scorching openmouthed kiss that left them both panting. He drew back and looked into her eyes, wanting to kiss her again, but he needed to settle things first.

He noticed the guards watching from the other end of the porch, both armed with rifles. Jack Bear Den stood beside Ray Strong. They nodded at Colt, Jack scowling and Ray smiling. It was hard to believe that the pair were such good friends, because they were different in almost every way.

Kacey's breath was returning to normal. "Would you like to go sit by the river?"

She was trying to gain them some privacy, or what little they could find and still be under the watchful eye of Tribal Thunder, the FBI and soon the Justice Department.

He offered to carry Charlie and she turned him over. He had missed the baby boy more than he cared to consider. If Kacey would not allow him along, he might lose them both. The thought tore him up like a cat clawing through cardboard.

She sat on the split log bench and he returned Charlie to her.

"He's bigger, isn't he?" Colt asked.

Kacey's smile was sunshine on a cloudy day. "I thought so, too. Lori took great care of him."

"How did things go with the FBI?" he asked.

"I didn't tell them who drove me. I said I didn't remember."

Colt snorted. "How did that go?"

Her stare was glassy. "They didn't believe me."

"Ty told me that they know anyway. They have the recording from my phone. It caught some of your conversation with Ty."

Kacey's head sank.

"You don't need to protect him," said Colt.

"Well, someone should," she said.

"What do you mean?"

"He takes care of things, really dangerous things, and he seems to always end up holding the bag. Why is that?"

Colt had never thought of it that way. He just needed help and Ty always gave it to him.

He had no answer, so he watched the river flow. It marked the time passing along between them. How could he convince her?

"They didn't find my friends," said Kacey.

"They still might," he said.

She looked down at Charlie, using her knuckle to stroke his cheek.

"I'm sorry I dragged you back into this," she said. "And for nothing."

"Kacey, you did all you could."

She blew away a breath. "I'm sure Marta has delivered by now. I'm so afraid that they'll find her body dumped somewhere, or worse, that they won't find it."

"Don't give up. They're all looking. Our tribe. The FBI. Someone will uncover something."

She met his gaze, searching. "Do you believe that?"

"I do."

Kacey nodded, her mouth tight. "All right, then."

"So you are going into witness relocation?" He

tried to sound casual, but his voice cracked. She noticed, giving him an odd stare. He saw a flicker of something, as if she were trying to puzzle something out.

"They don't think I have much of an option. They believe the Russians won't give up."

Colt understood that. Letting her live was bad for their reputation and their business. And there was no telling what else she might know about them. Details she might still recall.

"Permanent?" he asked.

Her gaze skittered from his and lifted up to the canyon beyond the river. Her swallow was audible and finally she nodded, a short rapid bobbing.

"Will they take me, too?" he asked.

Her gaze snapped to his. "What do you mean?"

"I want to go with you, Kacey."

"With me?" She was shaking her head now, reluctant, it seemed, to even consider the possibility.

His heart dropped down into the cavity below his chest and began banging around, like an animal suddenly falling into a pit.

"You can't. This is your home. Your brothers are here, your mother. My sisters are all living with her now, too. You should help her, be there for her."

"I want to be there for you."

"Colt, the only thing we ever argued over was my wish to leave the rez and your need to stay."

"I love you, Kacey," he said, thinking that explained everything.

She gave a long moan and was on her feet, swaying as if wanting to run but having nowhere to go.

"No, no, no," she whispered, lifting Charlie's head to her cheek and whispering the words. Tears overflowed her lower lids and dropped to the ground, coming faster as he watched.

He took hold of her shoulders, turning her to face him.

"Kacey, did you hear me? I love you."

"I heard," she said. "But you won't. You'll long for this place. It's a part of you, like your skin or your heart. You can't live without it."

"I want to go with you."

"You won't be able to come back."

"I understand that."

"It costs too much."

"That is my decision. All you need to tell me is if you love me, Kacey. If you love me, then we should be together."

The tears kept coming. Rolling along, one after another in a waterfall down her cheeks.

"You'll blame me," she whispered.

"Blame you? For what?"

"For what you have lost. For who you have lost." She looked at the ground. "You'll miss them. Your brothers. Your sister. Your mom."

"Of course I will."

"They'll hate me, too."

"It's not their decision. It's ours."

She wept into her hands.

"Kacey?" He used two fingers to lift her chin until their eyes met. "The only thing I cannot live without is you."

She broke into a sob and he pulled her tight, holding her in one arm and her baby in the other.

"Let me come with you, Kacey," he whispered, stroking her head. "Let me love you and marry you and be a father to Charlie. Let us build a life together away from the men who are hunting you. I'll be there to protect you and you will be my tribe and my people."

"Oh, Colt, it's so hard."

He rocked her, pressing his lips to her temple. "Not as hard as losing you."

He felt the moment of surrender, when her body sagged against his. He closed his eyes to offer a prayer of thanks.

"Will we be a family?" he asked.

"Oh, Colt, I wish you wouldn't do this."

"Because you love me?"

"Yes."

He drew back and smiled. Then he brushed his thumbs over her cheeks, wiping away the tears.

"Wonder where we'll go?" he asked, already looking forward.

"They are giving me a choice of several places."

"We should be married before we leave the rez," he said. "I'd like to have my family there for that."

"And mine. But I'm leaving tomorrow."

"We're leaving."

She nodded. "Yes, we."

Colt draped an arm around her shoulders and started them back toward the lodge. "Hope it's not Hawaii."

"Why is that?"

Colt nodded toward Jack Bear Den. "The detective is bringing his fiancée there to meet his father's people."

"I heard that. His dad was Hawaiian, right?"

"That's what they say. Explains a lot."

"Well, I doubt they'll send us there."

"Can you picture him on a surfboard?"

Kacey tried to imagine the massive man balancing on moving water and giggled. "Or with a ukulele?"

Now Colt was laughing. "I'd pay good money to see him in a grass skirt spinning a fire stick."

They reached the porch, side by side.

"Can you call Agent Forrest? There has been a change of plans," said Colt.

"What change?" asked Ray.

"We're getting married," said Colt.

Both Ray Strong and Jack Bear Den stared in dumb silence.

"They won't like that," said Ray at last.

"Call him," said Colt and walked Kacey inside to meet with Kenshaw. It was their shaman's opinion that they should be married before they told the Justice Department. Unlike out there, here on the rez they did not need a waiting period or blood tests or anything but a witness to their marriage.

They were married that evening before the fieldstone fireplace under the great seal of their people. Their shaman performed the ceremony before Colt's family and Kacey's sisters. Colt asked Ty to sign the certificate, and Kacey chose Hazel Trans. They presented the paperwork to the Justice Department the following morning. There was some pushback, but the marriage was valid, so accommodations were made.

"I wish you didn't have to leave Turquoise Canyon," said Kacey to Colt. "I know you love living here."

"I wasn't living, Kacey. Before you appeared, I was existing. You brought me back to my family. I'm whole again because of you. And I plan to spend every day of my life showing you what you mean to me."

They were transported to Phoenix. Colt thought he saw a familiar motorcycle following them down the mountain. He didn't mention this to anyone, but he did see a familiar face in the airport as they boarded their flight with their new identities six days later.

He did not know how Ty would figure out their connecting flights, but when Ty again appeared in the Seattle airport, disembarking from the same plane, Colt smiled. Colt had done nothing to jeopardize their new identity or their relocation. It was not his fault if his brother Ty was a better tracker than the Justice Department could have anticipated.

When they reached their final destination in Anchorage, Alaska, Colt glanced back to look for Ty. He did not see him, but somehow he believed he was still there.

"I'm already registered at the university," Kacey said, pointing out the campus on the map. "Spring semester. It's only a few miles from the house."

"Perfect," he said.

"You won't start work until the breakup," she said, meaning the time the river ice finally came crashing downriver and the fishing season could begin. "Will you be bored?"

They had arranged for Colt to work as a fishing and hunting guide with a local outfit. He had the skill set and would only need to get acclimatized to fishing for salmon rather than trout, bass and pike.

"I've got the little guy to take care of until then," he said. "When Mommy is in class."

"You mean Taylor," she said, trying on the new name they had assigned Charlie.

"That's right, Kalyn," he said and grinned at her.

"Almost there, Cash," she said.

Her husband held the door to the Jeep under the watchful eye of their escort in Anchorage. She stepped into the vehicle that would bring them to their new home.

"Seat belt, Mrs. Tsosie," said Colt.

Kacey complied as Colt strapped Charlie's car seat into the seat beside her. They had made a game of using their new names, to become used to them. Cash and Kalyn Tsosie and their newborn son, Taylor, headed for their new home and new life.

It was just one of many adjustments they would be making over the next few weeks. Their escort had told them that Tsosie was a somewhat common name among the native peoples here. That and their brown skin and black hair would help them blend, and if their features did not quite match those of the indigenous men and women of Alaska, it would be obvious only to the most observant.

Colt and Kacey traveled up a mountain road with sweeping views of the valley below in Anchorage. Finally the car slowed.

As she moved forward, Kacey thought back. She would not forget those they had left behind, but she would move forward into this new life with gratitude. Somehow through all the pain and loss, life had led her to what she had always desired.

Colt stared out at the window at the large A-frame home sitting off the road and up against the hillside.

"That can't be it," said Colt.

"It is," said the Justice Department agent in the front passenger seat.

Kacey smiled in delight. With Colt and Charlie, she would find what she had always wanted.

"Look at that," Colt said, his voice full of wonder.

"Yes," she said. "We're home."

* * * * *

Look out for the next book in
APACHE PROTECTORS: WOLF DEN,
UNDERCOVER SCOUT

Available next month!

Can't wait for more Jenna Kernan?
Check out her previous titles:

SURROGATE ESCAPE
TURQUOISE GUARDIAN
EAGLE WARRIOR
FIREWOLF

Available now from Harlequin Intrigue!

SPECIAL EXCERPT FROM

*Tucker Cahill returns to Gilt Edge, Montana,
with no choice but to face down his haunted past
when a woman's skeletal remains are found near
his family's ranch—but he couldn't have prepared
for a young woman seeking vengeance and
finding much more.*

*Read on for a sneak preview of
HERO'S RETURN,
A CAHILL RANCH NOVEL
from* New York Times *bestselling author
B.J. Daniels!*

Skeletal Remains Found in Creek

The skeletal remains of a woman believed to be in her late teens or early twenties were discovered in Miner's Creek outside of Gilt Edge, Montana, yesterday. Local coroner Sonny Bates estimated that the remains had been in the creek for somewhere around twenty years.

Sheriff Flint Cahill is looking into missing-persons cases from that time in the hopes of identifying the victim. If anyone has any information, they are encouraged to call the Gilt Edge Sheriff's Department.

"NO, MRS. KERN, I can assure you that the bones that were found in the creek are not those of your nephew Billy," Sheriff Flint Cahill said into the phone at his desk. "I saw Billy last week at the casino. He was alive and well… No, it takes longer than a week for a body to decompose to nothing but bones. Also, the skeletal remains that were found were a young woman's… Yes, Coroner Sonny Bates can tell the difference."

He looked up as the door opened and his sister, Lillie, stepped into his office. From the scowl on her face, he didn't have to ask what kind of mood she was in. He'd been expecting her, given that he had their father locked up in one of the cells.

"Mrs. Kern, I have to go. I'm sorry Billy hasn't called you, but I'm sure he's fine." He hung up with a sigh. "Dad's in the back sleeping it off. Before he passed out, he mumbled about getting back to the mountains."

A very pregnant Lillie nodded but said nothing. Pregnancy had made his sister even prettier. Her long dark hair framed a face that could only be called adorable. This morning, though, he saw something in her gray eyes that worried him.

He waited for her to tie into him, knowing how she felt about him arresting their father for being drunk and disorderly. This wasn't their first rodeo. And like always, it was Lillie who came to bail Ely out—not his bachelor brothers Hawk and Cyrus, who wanted to avoid one of Flint's lectures.

He'd been telling his siblings that they needed to

do something about their father. But no one wanted to face the day when their aging dad couldn't continue to spend most of his life in the mountains gold panning and trapping—let alone get a snoot full of booze every time he finally hit town again.

"I'll go get him," Flint said, lumbering to his feet. Since he'd got the call about the bones being found at the creek, he hadn't had but a few hours' sleep. All morning, the phone had been ringing off the hook. Not with leads on the identity of the skeletal remains—just residents either being nosy or worried there was a killer on the loose.

"Before you get Dad…" Lillie seemed to hesitate, which wasn't like her. She normally spoke her mind without any encouragement at all.

He braced himself.

"A package came for Tuck."

That was the last thing Flint had expected out of her mouth. "To the saloon?"

"To the ranch. No return address."

Flint felt his heart begin to pound harder. It was the first news of their older brother Tucker since he'd left home right after high school. Being the second oldest, Flint had been closer to Tucker than with his younger brothers. For years, he'd feared him dead. When Tuck had left like that, Flint had suspected his brother was in some kind of trouble. He'd been sure of it. But had it been something bad enough that Tucker hadn't felt he could come to Flint for help?

"Did you open the package?" he asked.

Lillie shook her head. "Hawk and Cyrus thought about it but then called me."

He tried to hide his irritation that one of them had called their sister instead of him, the darned sheriff. His brothers had taken over the family ranch and were the only ones still living on the property, so it wasn't a surprise that they would have received the package. Which meant that whoever had sent it either didn't know that Tucker no longer lived there or they thought he was coming back for some reason.

Because Tucker was on his way home? Maybe he'd sent the package and there was nothing to worry about.

Unfortunately, a package after all this time didn't necessarily bode well. At least not to Flint, who came by his suspicious nature naturally as a lawman. He feared it might be Tucker's last effects.

"I hope *you* didn't open it."

Lillie shook her head. "You think this means he's coming home?" She sounded so hopeful it made his heart ache. He and Tucker had been close in more ways than age. Or at least he'd thought so. But something had been going on with his brother his senior year in high school and Flint had no idea what it was. Or if trouble was still dogging his brother.

For months after Tucker left, Flint had waited for him to return. He'd been so sure that whatever the trouble was, it was temporary. But after all these years, he'd given up any hope. He'd feared he would never see his brother again.

"Tell them not to open it. I'll stop by the ranch and check it out."

Lillie met his gaze. "It's out in my SUV. I brought it with me."

Flint swore under his breath. What if it had a bomb in it? He knew that was overly dramatic, but still, knowing his sister... There wasn't a birthday or Christmas present that she hadn't shaken the life out of as she'd tried to figure out what was inside it. "Is your truck open?" She nodded. "Wait here."

He stepped out into the bright spring day. Gilt Edge sat in a saddle surrounded by four mountain ranges still tipped with snow. Picturesque, tourists came here to fish its blue-ribbon trout stream. But winters were long and a town of any size was a long way off.

Sitting in the middle of Montana, Gilt Edge also had something that most tourists didn't see. It was surrounded by underground missile silos. The one on the Cahill Ranch was renown because that was where their father swore he'd seen a UFO not only land, but also that he'd been forced on board back in 1967. Which had made their father the local crackpot.

Flint took a deep breath, telling himself to relax. His life was going well. He was married to the love of his life. But still, he felt a foreboding that he couldn't shake off. A package for Tucker after all these years?

The air this early in the morning was still cold, but there was a scent to it that promised spring wasn't that far off. He loved spring and summers here and had been looking forward to picnics, trail rides and finishing the yard around the house he and Maggie were building.

He realized that he'd been on edge since he'd got the call about the human bones found in the creek. Now he could admit it. He'd felt as if he was waiting for the other shoe to drop. And now this, he thought as he stepped to his sister's SUV.

The box sitting in the passenger-side seat looked battered. He opened the door and hesitated for a moment before picking it up. For its size, a foot-and-half-sized cube, the package was surprisingly light. As he lifted the box out, something shifted inside. The sound wasn't a rattle. It was more a rustle like dead leaves followed by a slight thump.

Like his sister had said, there was no return address. Tucker's name and the ranch address had been neatly printed in black—not in his brother's handwriting. The generic cardboard box was battered enough to suggest it had come from a great distance, but that wasn't necessarily true. It could have looked like that when the sender found it discarded and decided to use it to send the contents. He hesitated for a moment, feeling foolish. But he heard nothing ticking inside. Closing the SUV door, he carried the box inside and put it behind his desk.

"Aren't you going to open it?" Lilly asked, wide-eyed.

"No. You need to take Dad home." He started past his sister but vacillated. "I wouldn't say anything to him about this. We don't want to get his hopes up that Tucker might be headed home. Or make him worry."

She glanced at the box and nodded. "Did you ever understand why Tuck left?"

Flint shook his head. He was torn between anger and sadness when it came to his brother. Also fear. What had happened Tucker's senior year in high school? What if the answer was in that box?

"By the way," he said to his sister, "I didn't arrest Dad. Ely voluntarily turned himself in last night." He shrugged. Flint had never understood his father any more than he had his brother Tuck. To this day, Ely swore that he had been out by the missile silo buried in the middle of their ranch when a UFO landed, took him aboard and did experiments on him.

Then again, their father liked his whiskey and always had.

"You all right?" he asked his sister when she still said nothing.

Lillie nodded distractedly and placed both hands over the baby growing inside her. She was due any day now. He hoped the package for Tucker wasn't something that would hurt his family. He didn't want anything upsetting his sister in her condition. But he could see that just the arrival of the mysterious box had Lillie worried. She wasn't the only one.

TUCKER CAHILL SLOWED his pickup as he drove through Gilt Edge. He'd known it would be emotional, returning after all these years. He'd never doubted he would return—he just hadn't expected it to take nineteen years. All that time, he'd been waiting like a man on death row, knowing how it would eventually end.

Still, he was filled with a crush of emotion. *Home.* He hadn't realized how much he'd missed it, how much he'd missed his family, how much he'd missed his life in Montana. He'd been waiting for this day, dreading it and, at the same time, anxious to return at least once more.

As he started to pull into a parking place in front of the sheriff's department, he saw a pregnant woman come out followed by an old man with long gray hair and a beard. His breath caught. Not sure if he was more shocked to see how his father had aged—or how pregnant and grown up his little sister, Lillie, was now.

He couldn't believe it as he watched Lillie awkwardly climb into an SUV, the old man going around to the passenger side. He felt his heart swell at the sight of them. Lillie had been nine when he'd left. But he could never forget a face that adorable. Was that really his father? He couldn't believe it. When had Ely Cahill become an old mountain man?

He wanted to call out to them but stopped himself. As much as he couldn't wait to see them, there was something he had to take care of first. Tears burned his eyes as he watched Lillie drive their father away. It appeared he was about to be an uncle. Over the years while he was hiding out, he'd made a point of following what news he could from Gilt Edge. He'd missed so much with his family.

He swallowed the lump in his throat as he opened his pickup door and stepped out. The good news was that his brother Flint was sheriff. That, he hoped, would make it easier to do what he had to do. But facing Flint after all this time away… He knew he owed his family an explanation, but Flint more than the rest. He and his brother had been so close—until his senior year.

He braced himself as he pulled open the door to the sheriff's department and stepped in. He'd let everyone down nineteen years ago, Flint especially. He doubted his brother would have forgotten—or forgiven him.

But that was the least of it, Flint would soon learn.

AFTER HIS SISTER LEFT, Flint moved the battered cardboard box to the corner of his desk. He'd just pulled out his pocketknife to cut through the tape when his intercom buzzed.

"There's a man here to see you," the dispatcher said. He could hear the hesitation in her voice. "He says he's your *brother*?" His family members never had the dispatcher announce them. They just came on back to his office. *"Your brother, Tucker?"*

Flint froze for a moment. Hands shaking, he laid down his pocketknife as relief surged through him. Tucker was alive and back in Gilt Edge? He had to clear his throat before he said, "Send him in."

He told himself he wasn't prepared for this and yet it was something he'd dreamed of all these years. He stepped around to the front of his desk, half-afraid of what to expect. A lot could have happened to his brother in nineteen years. The big question, though, was why come back now?

As a broad-shouldered cowboy filled his office doorway, Flint blinked. He'd been expecting the worst.

Instead, Tucker looked great. Still undeniably handsome with his thick dark hair and gray eyes like the rest of the Cahills, Tucker had filled out from the teenager who'd left home. Wherever he'd been, he'd apparently fared well. He appeared to have been doing a lot of physical labor, because he was buff and tanned.

Flint was overwhelmed by both love and regret as he looked at Tuck, and furious with him for making him worry all these years.

"Hello, Flint," Tucker said, his voice deeper than Flint remembered.

He couldn't speak for a moment, afraid of what would come out of his mouth. The last thing he wanted to do was drive his brother away again. He wanted to hug him and slug him at the same time.

Instead, he said, voice breaking, "Tuck. It's so damned good to see you," and closed the distance between them to pull his older brother into a bear hug.

TUCKER HUGGED FLINT, fighting tears. It had been so long. Too long. His heart broke at the thought of the lost years. But Flint looked good, taller than Tucker remembered, broader shouldered, too.

"When did you get so handsome?" Tucker said as he pulled back, his eyes still burning with tears. It surprised him that they were both about the same height. Like him, Flint had filled out. With their dark hair and gray eyes, they could almost pass for twins.

The sheriff laughed. "You know darned well that you're the prettiest of the bunch of us."

Tucker laughed, too, at the old joke. It felt good. Just like it felt good to be with family again. "Looks like you've done all right for yourself."

Flint sobered. "I thought I'd never see you again."

"Like Dad used to say, I'm like a bad penny. I'm bound to turn up. How is the old man? Was that him I saw leaving with Lillie?"

"You didn't talk to them?" Flint sounded both surprised and concerned.

"I wanted to see you first." Tucker smiled as Flint laid a hand on his shoulder and squeezed gently before letting go.

"You know how he was after Mom died. Now he spends almost all of his time up in the mountains panning gold and trapping. He had a heart attack a while back, but it hasn't slowed him down. There's no talking any sense into him."

"Never was." Tucker nodded as a silence fell be-

tween them. He and Flint had once been so close.
Regret filled him as Flint studied him for a long moment before he stepped back and motioned him toward a chair in his office.

Closing the door, Flint settled into his chair behind his desk. Tucker dragged up one of the office chairs.

"I wondered if you wouldn't be turning up, since Lillie brought in a package addressed to you when she came to pick up Dad. He often spends a night in my jail when he's in town. Drunk and disorderly."

Tucker didn't react to that. He was looking at the battered brown box sitting on Flint's desk. *"A package?"* His voice broke. No one could have known he was coming back here unless…

Don't miss
HERO'S RETURN,
available March 2018 wherever
HQN Books and ebooks are sold.

www.Harlequin.com

COMING NEXT MONTH FROM
H HARLEQUIN®

INTRIGUE

Available April 17, 2018

#1779 COWBOY'S REDEMPTION
The Montana Cahills • by B.J. Daniels
Former army pilot Colt McCloud never forgot the woman he rescued over
a year ago. Now back home on his Montana ranch, Colt discovers
Lola Dayton on his doorstep...and learns that their baby girl has been
kidnapped.

#1780 ONE INTREPID SEAL
Mission: Six • by Elle James
After rescuing Reese Brantley in the Congo, can Navy SEAL "Diesel"
Dalton Samuel Landon avoid getting them both abducted by warring
factions—and at the same time not lose his heart to the beautiful bodyguard?

#1781 FINDING THE EDGE
Colby Agency: Sexi-ER • by Debra Webb
With a target on her back thanks to a vengeful gang leader, nurse
Eva Bowman turns to the Colby Agency for protection. Can she trust
investigator Todd Christian with her life—even if he once broke her young,
vulnerable heart?

#1782 UNDERCOVER SCOUT
Apache Protectors: Wolf Den • by Jenna Kernan
Tribal police detective Ava Hood has every intention of bringing down a
surrogacy ring. Then she learns all roads lead to Dr. Kee Redhorse's clinic,
and her attraction to the sexy physician becomes a lot more complicated...

#1783 ENDANGERED HEIRESS
Crisis: Cattle Barge • by Barb Han
A heartbreaking loss brings rancher Hudson Dale home to Cattle Barge,
where he crosses paths with Madelyn Kensington. Thanks to the terms of a
will, the beautiful stranger has become a target, giving Hudson the chance
at redemption he desperately craves.

#1784 THE SHERIFF'S SECRET
Protectors of Cade County • by Julie Anne Lindsey
When Tina Ellet's infant daughter is abducted, Sheriff West Garrett vows to
save the child, capture the criminal and prove to Tina that their love is worth
fighting for.

———————

HICNM0418

Get 2 Free Books,
Plus 2 Free Gifts —
just for trying the Reader Service!

HARLEQUIN
INTRIGUE

"I had nowhere else to go." Her words came out in a rush. "I was so
worried that you wouldn't be here." She burst into tears and slumped
as if physically exhausted.

He caught her, swung her up into his arms and carried her into the
house, kicking the door closed behind him. His mind raced as he tried
to imagine what could have happened to bring her to his door in Gilt
Edge, Montana, in the middle of the night and in this condition.

"Sit here," he said as he carried her in and set her down in a kitchen
chair before going for the first-aid kit. When he returned, he was
momentarily taken aback by the memory of this woman the first time
he'd met her. She wasn't beautiful in the classic sense. But she was
striking, from her wide violet eyes fringed with pale lashes to the silk
of her long blond hair. She had looked like an angel, especially in the
long white dress she'd been wearing that night.

That was over a year ago and he hadn't seen her since. Nor had he
expected to since they'd met initially several hundred miles from the
ranch. But whatever had struck him about her hadn't faded. There was
something flawless about her—even as scraped up and bruised as she
was. It made him furious at whoever was responsible for this.

"Can you tell me what happened?" he asked as he began to clean
the cuts.

"I...I..." Her throat seemed to close on a sob.

"It's okay, don't try to talk." He felt her trembling and could see that she was fighting tears. "This cut under your eye is deep."

She said nothing, looking as if it was all she could do to keep her eyes open. He took in her torn and filthy dress. It was long, like the white one he'd first seen her in, but faded. It reminded him of something his grandmother might have worn to do housework in. She was also thinner than he remembered.

As he gently cleaned her wounds, he could see dark circles under her eyes, and her long braided hair was in disarray with bits of twigs and leaves stuck in it.

The night he'd met her, her plaited hair had been pinned up at the nape of her neck—until he'd released it, the blond silk dropping to the center of her back.

He finished his doctoring, put away the first-aid kit and wondered how far she'd come to find him and what she had been through to get here. When he returned to the kitchen, he found her standing at the back window, staring out. As she turned, he saw the fear in her eyes—and the exhaustion.

Colt desperately wanted to know what had happened to her and how she'd ended up on his doorstep. He hadn't even thought that she'd known his name. "Have you had anything to eat?"

"Not in the past forty-eight hours or so," she said, squinting at the clock on the wall as if not sure what day it was. "And not all that much before that."

He'd been meaning to get into Gilt Edge and buy some groceries. "Sit and I'll see what I can scare up," he said as he opened the refrigerator. Seeing only one egg left, he said, "How do you feel about pancakes? I have chokecherry syrup."

She nodded and attempted a smile. She looked skittish as a newborn calf. Worse, he sensed that she was having second thoughts about coming here.

She licked her cracked lips. "I have to tell you. I have to explain—"

"It's okay. You're safe here."

Don't miss
COWBOY'S REDEMPTION by B.J. Daniels,
available May 2018 wherever
Harlequin Intrigue® books and ebooks are sold.

www.Harlequin.com

HIEXP0418

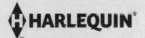

LOVE
Harlequin
romance?

Join our Harlequin community to share your thoughts and connect with other romance readers!

Be the first to find out about promotions, news, and exclusive content!

Sign up for the Harlequin e-newsletter and download a free book from any series at

www.TryHarlequin.com

CONNECT WITH US AT:

Harlequin.com/Community

 Facebook.com/HarlequinBooks

Twitter.com/HarlequinBooks

Instagram.com/HarlequinBooks

Pinterest.com/HarlequinBooks

ReaderService.com

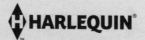 **HARLEQUIN**®

**ROMANCE WHEN
YOU NEED IT**

HSOCIAL2017

THE WORLD IS BETTER WITH

Romance

Harlequin has everything from contemporary, passionate and heartwarming to suspenseful and inspirational stories.

Whatever your mood, we have a romance just for you!

Reward the book lover in you!

Earn points from all your Harlequin book purchases from wherever you shop.

Turn your points into *FREE BOOKS* of your choice
OR
EXCLUSIVE GIFTS from your favorite authors or series.

Join for FREE today at
www.HarlequinMyRewards.com.

Harlequin My Rewards is a free program (no fees) without any commitments or obligations.

MYR17